ALSO BY JOHN CASEY

An American Romance

TESTIMONY

AND

DEMEANOR

TESTIMONY AND DEMEANOR

by John Casey

ALFRED A. KNOPF   NEW YORK   1979

Library of Congress Cataloging in Publication Data

Casey, John.   Testimony and demeanor.

I. Title.
PZ4.C33934Te   1979   [PR6053.A79]   823'.9'14   78-20599
ISBN 0-394-50097-0

Manufactured in the United States of America

CONTENTS

A MORE COMPLETE
CROSS-SECTION

WHEN I FIRST HEARD THAT I WAS TO go on active duty in the Army—specifically at Fort Knox, Kentucky—I welcomed the news. I regarded the ensuing six months' military service as an opportunity to see a more complete cross-section of my fellow man.

I was cheated at first. There were only surfaces. The people circled me like the moon the earth, always presenting the same face, keeping the dark side hidden.

Moreover, the shock of being suddenly piled together in Fort Knox distorted even the surface appearances; I saw them as though through a prismatic kaleidoscope, their true colors and shapes scattered. No one was in his natural setting. I don't know why I had expected at least some of the people to be at home, but I could see that they were not—just by the way they fingered their stiff fatigue uniforms and ran their hands fitfully over their shaved heads. One man fainted when they clipped off his hair. That was interesting, but he disappeared from the reception center. There was only the prevailing fabric of the Army that held steady. That, however, was somewhat more richly textured than I had imagined. When I arrived at Fort Knox, the commanding general's name was Wonder. General Wonder. There were a number of coincidences of name, all of them equally hauntingly unperceived. The master sergeant who lectured us on military courtesy, company formations, and the meaning of bugle calls was named Roland. The supply sergeant who came to supervise us while we dyed our brown government-issue boots with black government-issue dye was named Glissen. If we had been asked to paint white roses red, I could not have been more delighted.

The first week of basic training we continued to be rushed about. There was always a great flurry, but our roles were so undemanding and passive that it was soothing. I did note that we had an apparently authentic sergeant. He was small and thin, with a rather unpleasant, fair—almost hairless—face.

"My name is McQueen," he said, underlining his name tag with the chewed end of his cigar. "My first name is Sergeant." He walked down the front row, looking up into our faces, and stopped in front of the boy next to me. "Ellridge," he said, reading the name tag in front of his nose.

"Yes, sir," Ellridge said.

"Don't call me 'sir.' I earn my money."

"All right." Ellridge was a Southerner with a soft agreeable voice.

McQueen spun on his heel and whistled. I turned to look at Ellridge while the sergeant's back was turned. His thin neck drooped forward as he watched McQueen with puzzlement. McQueen, facing him again, reached out. I rolled my eyes to watch. His fingers grasped the middle button of Ellridge's fatigue shirt. The button was unbuttoned. In the sergeant's belt buckle I could see the reflection of Ellridge's left hand as it moved. I turned and saw him cover the top of his own left thigh with it.

"You're pretty sloppy, Ellridge. Do you really want that button?"

Ellridge smiled nervously.

McQueen ripped it off. "You'd better sew it on, then," he said.

"I could have just buttoned it," Ellridge said.

McQueen stared at him. Then his eyes lighted on Ellridge's left hand. "What's your hand doing there, Ellridge? You going to play with yourself?"

There was general laughter. Ellridge looked at me with dismay, and I looked curiously at McQueen.

He stared back at me. "What're you staring at, troop? You want to get in on it too?"

There was more laughter.

"You better get your eyes front!" he said, grunting the last word so that it had a rather attractive nasal resonance.

But he also disappeared. The first sergeant told me that he

had been flown to Walter Reed Hospital on compassionate leave to be with his Korean stepdaughter while she had an eye operation.

First Sergeant Plisetsky was a large man. His chest was at least fifty inches around, as were his waist and hips. He invited me to his office at Company HQ. He told me McQueen was gone and that there was no one in charge of my barracks. He invited me to sit down.

"I see you smoke cigars," he said, pointing to the large flat tin in my breast pocket. I offered him one. He took the tin and said with benevolence, "Have one yourself." We puffed in silence. "You didn't get these at the PX," he said, handing me back the package.

"No," I answered.

"Very fine," he said, "very fine. I like cigars. Kipling liked cigars. I like Kipling too."

"Yes," I said.

"So you used to wrestle up at college," he said, tapping my 201 file with his finger. "Fine sport. That why you dropped R.O.T.C.?"

"In a way."

"I understand," he said. "It's all right."

He reached in a drawer of his desk and pulled out a navy-blue brassard with three chevrons on it and handed it to me. "This is just field stripes," he said. "No pay." He paused and then added with satisfaction, "But that won't bother you."

I pinned the brassard on with the safety pins hanging from the worn felt.

He sighed. "I used to be first sergeant for a training company of clerk-typists. They used to play bridge. You don't play bridge, do you? I thought we could get up a foursome. I often spend the night here," he said, pointing to the cot behind him. "I'm a bachelor."

"No," I said.

"The best bridge player I ever met was a Harvard man too.

Big fellow, dark hair. But that was some years back. You wouldn't know him."

We smoked awhile.

"You won't have to stand guard, or do any KP," he said. "But try to stop the fighting. They're lonely, they're nervous, they're"—he stopped to knock a cigar ash into the saucer of his coffee cup—"pent up. We used to run. Even my clerk-typists used to run. If they run, they just go to bed. But we can't run anymore while it's warm. A boy died of heat stroke running up a hill. More likely it was a weak heart. Not in our regiment, but still we can't run. So try to control the horseplay in the barracks. I'll stop by before the evening meal and tell them you're the platoon guide. As far as they're concerned, you're just like a sergeant." He started to sigh again but yawned. "It's not so bad. Not so bad as they all say. I do my job. You do your job. We all do a job. You'll all be gone soon."

I went slightly and pleasantly mad during the next three weeks. The sun shone through the dust in such a mysterious way that I could not believe what we were all doing. I had looked forward to the time in the Army as one of disembodied observation, but I found I still couldn't see the people as I had hoped. It was arranged that we rarely talked, but I also couldn't see them because the sun only seemed to shine on things. I saw the black high gloss on the rows of boot tips melt into dullness under the sun. I saw sweat spreading across the softened fibers of fatigue shirts, squeezed out from under the suspenders of the pack harness. I saw hands groping with pieces of rifle. Interminably. And I was dazzled by looking at my shiny thumbnail through the bores of all their rifles. When I looked down the spirals, I had no idea how far away the other end was. I could feel my left hand around the barrel, and I could see my right thumbnail flicking the sunlight at my eye—but sometimes so close it was only the distance through a keyhole, sometimes so far that my stomach lunged up to my chest. Pleasurably, I think. It was a beautiful sight—the glistening foreshortened rifling—and I was often hypnotized.

The roads we walked on were sometimes soft. The asphalt gave off colorless heat waves reminiscent of the beams in the rifle barrel, but the road itself was velvet, velvet gray as it climbed the hill ahead of us toward the sun.

I was a half ghost when the sun went down. I could not tell the men from shadows then. There was nothing to do. It seemed a profanation of the place to read. I could hear voices calling to each other. "Him? He don't care. Just as long as your shit don't smell." There were also many small radios that tissue-papered a song—"Come-a come-a come-a come-a to me"—while steam poured out of the shower room, through the latrine (bearing with it the smell of mentholated shaving cream), and out the double screen doors in the flank of the barracks.

Every night my bunkmate—Demry McGlaughlin was his name—asked me softly, "Is anything wrong, man?"

"No," I said. It startled me every time.

What was wrong was—perhaps was—that I knew I made up so much of each day and yet I felt the shadow of all their minds pass over it. I did not know whether they were drawn into my imagination or whether I was drawn into seeing what they saw. Whichever it was, it was a great strain. To be sure, when they slept I was released. As soon as they closed their eyes, I felt the bloat of my authority subside. I was alone, and I saw only what concerned me. I alone saw the moon shine on the white foot powder on the floor, as soft as flour on a pantry table. I saw the moonlight—on the pronged silver knob of the drinking fountain, gleaming hard at a great distance from my open eye. In the morning I felt good. I used to sing as I bloused my fatigue pants. Once someone said behind my back, "What's he singing about—all the crap he's gonna give us?"

I said out loud without turning, "I don't think you've

thought very carefully about what you said. The chair gives you leave to reconsider."

Usually I ignored who said what. There were so few freedoms for them that I thought they should at least have the freedom of speech. The only way they could be sure of it was by my perfect impartiality, and perfect impartiality is ignorance.

Demry chuckled. He was the only one in the barracks appreciably bigger than I.

I favored him. Otherwise I was fair. I favored him not because he was the biggest, nor because he was a Negro, but because he was the first to emerge. I saw him speaking to me and heard him, both at once.

In general, my reaction to the swell of voices within the barracks was like the sort of puzzlement one has watching a flock of birds, hearing them call to each other but being unable to associate a particular call with a particular bird. As a consequence I could never address anyone by name unless he was wearing a clean name tag and happened to be standing within reading distance and facing me. However, on several occasions I called the roll at assembly entirely from memory. But I knew Demry. Demry was like a large crow flapping along from tree to tree in plain sight, cawing down at me, sometimes companionably, sometimes derisively, but always clearly. That may have been because he seemed to be humoring me. He laughed quite a lot.

What I said fell heavily on the others. I sometimes would say whatever I was thinking and it dismayed them, especially since the first sergeant often appeared to tell them that he stood behind whatever *I* told them. Thus, a number of lyric and scientific observations became curiously embedded in my impersonation of a sergeant, the whole batch of which was repeatedly stamped with approval by the first sergeant. I could also say "InspickSHUNNN . . . HARums!" Click. Click. Clickety-

click. "You min *will* do that again and you min *will* do it
ERRIGHT!" as well as some other things along that line.

But those were only the ornaments and accidents of my
efforts; the substance was plain and just. Their hours in the
barracks were arranged on concentric cardboard wheels that I
set each morning after breakfast. In the field the first sergeant's
voice reached us all on every main question. I believed no one
had reason to complain.

Yet there was fighting. The first time it was two very small
people. Demry held one and I the other. We put them under
the shower. The second time it was somewhat larger people,
but after a blow had been struck on each side someone saw a
plump nurse from the dental clinic walking slowly past the
barracks. The crowd rushed to line the roads. The two men
fighting became puzzled, and then alarmed. They left off fighting. One man—not one of the two—went on sick call with a
swollen knee. He had been pushed down the wooden steps on
the way out.

Sometimes things happened quickly. But mostly time was
quicker. The usual day would be half gone before anything of
substance came along. We moved very slowly from point to
point,—both while walking and while learning our rudiments.
There was a special stillness about the faces and postures of all
the people in the company—gathered outside the mess hall,
inside a classroom, on the roadside—that gave me the feeling
that they had been told they were being used as models for a
laborious and richly detailed mural painting. Even when we
were marching it seemed so—especially in the woods when a
bird or a squirrel would appear and disappear at a natural
speed. There was so much time passing that I could watch the
sun's shadow move from one side of a nose to the other. But
sometimes things happened quickly. One late afternoon we left
the company formation, trooped through the barracks, and
were seated outside cleaning rifles before the dust had settled

on the assembly area, a hundred yards away, visible from the wooden steps of our side porch. A few people stayed inside, but most of the platoon, stripped to their white T-shirts, were gathered on the ground in groups of three or four, their dog tags clanking gently as they slowly moved their forearms about, pulling apart their rifles with the peaceful rhythm of sheep tugging at clumps of grass. I went inside to drink at the water fountain. Demry was sitting on his bunk. I heard Ellridge ask him for the bore cleaner. Demry ignored him. He asked again. Demry said, "You'll get it. You'll get it. Just get off my back, boy."

Ellridge giggled loudly. I was surprised.

"Something funny?" Demry said. "You think that's funny? You go on and *tell* me what's funny, boy."

Ellridge said, "Oh, *you* know." His eyelids drooped almost languidly. But when he looked up again his eyes were wide, his mouth parted, and his cheeks sucked in with fear. I began to see the point about "boy." It was astonishing how quickly they had come to the point, without a word of elaboration, without having anything else in common. Even so, I would have thought Demry was being overly subtle, but I could see Ellridge's response of coyness and panic. And there *is* something about ineptness—ineptness at daring as well as ineptness at flight—that arouses loathing and aggression.

"You better say something, boy," Demry said.

Ellridge looked over at me and gave another nervous laugh. "I don't have to talk to you," he said to Demry.

There were ten men in from the steps before Ellridge finished answering. They loved a fight. They probably smelled it when he opened his mouth the first time. We hadn't had a real fight for a week. Demry got up and moved toward Ellridge. The men moved closer until they were packed tight in a ring. They knew I was behind them and that I was supposed to break it up. More men came in and squeezed around.

It was disgusting how terrified Ellridge looked. I was surprised when he began to move his mouth again and said, with great effort, "I don't have to talk to you." It was like a turtle laying eggs—a quick nervous convulsion for each word, the eyes blinking slowly, out of phase with the movements of his mouth.

Ellridge backed up, but then he laughed again. The laugh was out of control and dragged up an ugly whimper at the end. He hiccuped. It would have been funny except for Demry's bulk leaning forward. Ellridge's hands flew out to steady himself. One hand against the wall, the other against the rifle rack.

Demry said, "I'm gonna make you quit laughing, boy."

One of the men in the front row called out, "He's not gonna fight him—he's gonna rape him!"

Attacked by their laughter, Ellridge pulled an M-1 from the rack. For an instant I was afraid he might have smuggled a cartridge back from the range, but he came to a kind of high port arms and said, "Don't you come near me—I'll split your head." He waggled the butt of the rifle. Demry grabbed an end of the iron locking bar and pulled it out of the last slot, from which it had been jutting askew. It trailed by his foot for an instant. He seemed to swing it lightly, but the rifle jumped two feet in the air. Ellridge jumped back into the corner as it fell. There was a notch in the side of the stock in front of the trigger housing. I'd hate to think it was the sight of damage to government property that moved me, but it was then that I pushed aside the people in front of me. I called to Demry. He turned.

"He's a good deal smaller than you are," I said. "You could break him into pieces. You know that. But we couldn't put him back together, you know. . . ."

Demry looked at me meditatively.

"Do you want him to apologize?" I asked.

"No," he said, and handed me the locking bar. He walked back to his bunk, sat down, and held the barrel of his rifle up to his eye, pointing the other end at the window as though he were looking at the sky with a telescope.

"Get out," I said to the others. They really were terrible bloodsuckers sometimes.

"Not you," I said, somewhat unnecessarily, to Ellridge, who was still standing in the corner. The others sluggishly passed out the double door. Ellridge put the rifle back and followed me out the front door. We went around to the furnace-room side of the barracks. I leaned against the side of the building, wondering for a moment what people thought of Ellridge where he came from. Did life there go on in such simple harmony that it didn't matter what they thought—that whatever he was was all that anyone hoped for him? Leave him to his same old tune. Or were people there distressed at weakness too? He should at least try to turn out all right. He stood facing me. When I finally spoke, he suddenly checked the buttons to the flaps of his shirt pockets.

I said, "It might seem unfair to you but I wish you would stay away from McGlaughlin. Don't talk to him. Don't get in his way. In fact, don't even put yourself next to him in formation."

"It was the colored boy started it."

"His name is McGlaughlin," I said. "And who started it doesn't matter. This is just to maintain the peace—like the United States keeping Chiang Kai-shek from overrunning China."

But that was just part of my old tune. He didn't listen to it.

"They said it would be a lot worse," he said softly. "Back home they said that."

"It's not so bad, then," I concluded hopefully. "And it should get better for all of us. It's not so long now."

I also defended them. One night, long after lights out, a newly assigned member of the company cadre intruded. At that time he held the rank of specialist fourth class. When I woke up, he was shining a flashlight on a pile of foot powder on the floor and demanding that it be swept up.

I got out of bed and went over. Ellridge was sleepily refusing to get up, and the specialist, whose name was Shoemaker, brayed at him more and more noisily.

"Jesus, Ellridge, why is it always you?" I said. "Never mind, never mind...."

"You get back in the rack," Shoemaker said, shining the light in my eyes.

I put my hand over the lens, saying, "Don't shine the light in my eyes."

"Don't get lively, Bonzo. You're in the Army now. You touch me and they'll lock you up."

"You're making an awful lot of noise. Why don't you step outside and discuss sweeping the floor in the morning?"

"Who the hell are you?" he asked.

"He's the sergeant," Ellridge said.

"The hell he is," Shoemaker replied.

"I have field stripes, I think they're called."

"Field rank don't mean diddly, Bonzo."

"Doesn't," I said. "But I think it does."

"You come with me," Shoemaker insisted. "You come with me and you'll find out what's what." I turned to get my clothes. "You just come as you are. You won't get frostbite."

I ignored him. He turned back to Ellridge. "That better be off the floor when I get back."

He followed me down to my end of the barracks and, while I dressed, took the lid off the trash barrel. "This place is a pigsty," he said, peering in. He shone his light on Demry in the lower bunk. "You go dump this in the dumpster." Demry rolled over. I pulled my boots on without lacing them and went out the side door. Shoemaker followed me; he didn't want me to get to Sergeant Plisetsky first. Yet when we got to the HQ he didn't want to be the one to wake him. He invited me to. I declined.

"They're going to crucify you," he said. He put his flashlight down on the desk sharply. Then he pulled open a drawer and dropped it in. Sergeant Plisetsky rolled onto his back, crossed his forearms on his stomach like flippers, and exhaled at length. He looked very comfortable. Shoemaker opened a drawer very quietly. He took up a pencil and, looking up at my name tag several times, wrote my name down on a note pad.

"I've got your name," he said, tapping it with his forefinger.

"Well done!" I said.

"I've had about enough out of you, Bonzo. Now get out. Get out of here before I put my boot so far up your ass you won't be able to tell shit from Shinola."

I put my finger to my lips and nodded toward the sleeping First Sergeant.

Shoemaker contrived a number of small inconveniences immediately after that. I think he held up some mail for a while. For example, my weekly tin of Danish cigars was late, and a little stale. But, without becoming threatened directly, he was cured of being a bother at night.

It suddenly turned cold two days before we went on our bivouac. I liked the feel of the ground turning hard. I'd never been so constantly exposed to the countryside during a change of season. In the same cubic yard of air that was warm one afternoon you could see your breath the next. The C.O.'s jeep took a wrong turn when wheel ruts in what had been simply a damp intersection became as intransigent as railroad switches. The leaves on the ground were no longer soft and colored but shriveled up, in plain brown rigor mortis. Dull as wrapping paper. It was the evergreens that grew darker and richer. And the stars grew brighter, especially as the moon waned.

We pitched our tents in rows on top of a ridge. The iron tent pegs were the only ones that went in successfully. There was a good deal of muttering when I asked those with iron pegs to share them with those with wooden ones, so they could at least start their holes. It was as though the cold withered their small patches of generosity as it had the leaves. Of course, most of them were sick too. When the weather changed, First Sergeant Plisetsky had us run, and the sweat chilled on them when they would lie down during the breaks.

The first night on bivouac it was our platoon's chore to post a sentry every two hours of the night. Demry drew two to four and Ellridge four to six—the last two watches. As we sat outside our tent smoking, Demry didn't seem to mind either the cold or his assignment. From the ridge we could see the blinking light on top of the hospital, the tallest building in Fort Knox. It was seven miles away. We could hear the firing from the artillery range in between the gusts of wind, but we couldn't see the flashes.

"There's a shooting star," he said.

"Maybe it was a flare," I said. "Or an airplane landing."

"No. It was a shooting star. I know shooting stars all right." He lay back. "Just look at those stars. There must be thousands of them. Hundreds of miles away."

I laughed.

"What's so funny?"

"To begin with, there're not thousands of them but millions. More likely billions. And they're not hundreds of miles away. Most of them are so far they have to be measured in light-years. A light-year is the distance that light travels in a year."

"Where'd they teach you that? At college?"

"No. I don't know. I learned it here and there. Like the names of birds . . ."

"Uh-huh," he said.

"Or the names of football teams."

"You know all that too. That's real good."

I said nothing.

"You still didn't tell me what's the funny part," he said.

I answered hastily, "Look—if I had asked, 'Who's Joe

Louis?' or—or anyone. Elvis Presley. You would have found that funny."

"Uh-huh. I bet you know all about Joe Louis, though. I don't think I could tell you a thing about Joe Louis. We *all* know about Joe Louis."

Again I said nothing, although I thought how unfair it was that each slip of my tongue should have been misinterpreted just enough to keep the chance to explain slightly beyond my reach. It also occurred to me that he was deliberately taking advantage of my inexperience in a worse way than I had unwittingly offended his.

We went to sleep without saying anything else. At two o'clock the sentry reached between the buttons on the front flaps and shook my foot. "McGlaughlin, you're on," he said, and left. I made a note of that. The sentry was supposed to wait until his relief was on his feet and clearly awake. But then, he might have been afraid of Demry. Or he might have waked me on purpose. I tried not to think that. Having only recently overcome my inability to see these people, I didn't want to swing to the other extreme of paranoia.

I shook Demry's shoulder. He sat up. I could hear his head scraping the top of the tent.

"What time is it?" he asked.

"Two. You're on guard duty."

"Two o'clock in the morning?" he said.

"Yes."

"Two o'clock in the morning."

"That's right."

"Man, that's my bedtime." He lay down again.

"Someone's got to be on guard."

"I'll just guard everything right here."

"Come on, Demry," I said, laughing.

"You go on and laugh," he said. "I'm staying right here. It's cold out there."

"Someone's got to be on guard duty."

"You're someone. You may have forgot that."

"Look, Demry. You know as well as I do that the only way this whole thing can work is if everyone takes his turn. You have to have turns. That's the only way discipline can be imposed and still be fair."

He sat up again. "You're very big on discipline, man. And you know why? It's because you don't really live here. You don't live here at all. You get out of here and you go home. You know, home. That place where they send you magazines from. And those little cigars. *That's* right—you got it—home. Where you live. But get this—I live here. I am here and you are not." I could hear his rapid breathing as he paused. "So as long as I'm *here,* I'm not going to get sick or go crazy over your rules. You have it nice and easy, right? And if I sleep right alongside you a little of that is going to rub off. So we're just going to skip walking around out there. . . ." He lay down. I didn't say anything. "I'll tell you," he continued. "You may know a hell of a lot of things, but one thing you do *not* know is how to get *me* out *there.*"

I got out from under my blankets and knelt on top of them. I thought awhile. "Would you stand guard for me?" I asked.

He exhaled with his teeth closed. "I'm not going to talk all night, man." He turned over. "O.K. I'll tell you," he said in a more moderate way. "If it was me, I'd roll over and not give a damn. If I was you, I'd say, 'Demry baby, have yourself a good sleep!' "

"O.K.," I said, and put my clothes on. "I'll do it for you," I said, and unbuttoned the flaps, crawled out with my rifle and boots, and pulled my field jacket with the chevrons on it through the hole behind me as though it were a soul leaving a body.

The stars were very bright. It really did look as though they might be not so far away—even as though it were the wind that was fanning them into a fiercer glow. I wondered if Demry thought that stars were cold.

I walked in zigzags down the bare slope to the nearest pine trees and waited. It finally occurred to me that no matter what happened while I was in the Army, I would not really be changed—not the way I was by school or college. I was no longer being formed. All I could have from now on were sensations, which would be absorbed and digested by the way I already was. I cast my thoughts back to where my real life was going on. Where it was being considered, planned, felt. Where it was carefully creeping forward. When I would catch up with it. Way stations, rungs, nests, and resting places. Here I was a swallow flying through a long barn. A swallow among bats.

Yet I was still a little deranged. The pine trees were very clear to me. I went and touched them, their straight needles and their unknotted trunks, not as cold as I thought they would be, or as cold as I was.

I walked back up to the rows of tents. I didn't hear the wind, I was so used to it. The startling noise was the coughing. From one tent at a time it came—no particular sequence to it, no set interval. As the time passed, it seemed to me I was tending one large beast that was making its noises into the night.

At ten past four I looked at my watch. I went to wake Ellridge. They had only three buttons on their front flaps. I unhooked the loop and pulled it up. The buttons came out of the worn holes. Ellridge was sitting in the back, his knees to his chest, his blanket pulled around his shoulders. He looked like a monkey crouched in an outside cage in wintertime. He hadn't taken his boots off. How unfair it is, I thought, to add my order to the Army's. They suffer enough. I was about to put the flap down again when Ellridge spoke. "I'm not asleep," he said.

"O.K. On your feet." I said it by instinct.

He came out with his blanket around his shoulders. "How come McGlaughlin isn't on guard?"

"Look—I'm tired. It's my bedtime. Enough of this chit-chat. Get your field jacket on and start walking around."

"I thought you didn't have to do any of this guard."

He was exultant in a strange way, his eyes wide open and his mouth emitting little explosions—"ha! ah! oh!"—as though he had caught me doing something surprisingly daring and bad. He sucked in his breath, partly meaningfully and partly because he discovered how cold it was.

"You were covering up. You were covering up so he could stay wrapped up. That's right. The middle of the night. Then you came to get me up so you can crawl back in there. So you can crawl back into your hole alongside that— I didn't say it. I didn't say it, but I'll say it if you make me. If you make me stand out here with you crawling in there. But I will say it—oh, God, I will."

"Ellridge, will you get your rifle and stop gibbering."

"Oh, no. No, I won't! I thought you was somebody pretty good, you know that? I thought you was all right. I thought you was something special, but Lord, you're a sorry thing. You're a nigger-lover! Nothing else at all. That's all you do is just care for that nigger. That's all you do is love him. Is love him and kiss him . . ."

"I can't begin to tell you how stupid you are, Ellridge."

He looked at the sky, as though he could see the wind in it. Then he tucked his nose under the edge of his blanket and began to cry.

"O.K., Ellridge. Get back inside."

He stood there. I took him by the shoulders and turned him toward the tent. "Wait," he said.

We waited until he stopped crying. Then he stooped down and crawled back into the tent. I pulled the loop of the flap down over the peg and left while he was doing up the buttons.

I wanted to go down to the pine trees again, but I stayed by the tents. I wasn't tempted either to call Ellridge or to go into my tent and sleep. I couldn't face either of them. I was tempted to go lie down among the pine trees, but instead I tried to resist the wind. I tried to imagine that it was blowing right through me—so cleanly and so fast that it didn't hurt. That worked for a while. Then I couldn't keep imagining well enough, and I began to endure every minute, looking at my watch too often.

During the breaks the next day I had to lie down. I didn't seem to be sweating very much, so I thought it would be all right. Each time I lay down I thought of how when we got back for the night I would gather blanketfuls of pine needles to put under me, and even around me.

We stayed out late. And even though I knew I would be warmer with the pine needles, I didn't get them. I crawled into the tent and lay down. Demry went to sleep. I was about to fall asleep too when I felt a hand on my foot. I sat up expectantly, but no one said, "McGlaughlin, you're on." There was no one there. I lay awake alternately shivering and burning, trying to command my body to be calm. It is possible, but I couldn't bring myself to the right pitch to do it.

First Sergeant Plisetsky noticed that I wasn't myself the next day, and sent me on sick call. I was grateful. Everyone else was jealous. Demry thought I was lucky too. I had given in to so much by then that I even complained to him—explaining in a collapsed way that I had stood two watches.

"Well, you'll get to make it all up now," he said. There was something in his tone that I couldn't decipher. I thought he still considered me lucky, although I hoped he meant it encouragingly. They didn't take people into the infirmary with less than a hundred and one.

I got out of the hospital in only three days, but the company had already returned to the barracks, a day ahead of schedule. Shoemaker had been put in charge of the fourth platoon in my absence. He came up to me while I was sitting on my bunk cleaning my rifle. He had brand-new sergeant's stripes sewn on his fatigues. The distinction is between field rank and acting rank. Acting rank you may sew on.

"Did you have a nice rest?" he said, simpering. "We missed you. Yes, all of the boys really missed you, Bonzo."

"It was great," I said. "The nurses all loved me."

Demry laughed.

"Ooh, I don't know what we can do about that," Shoemaker said. "But I'll tell all the boys to try real hard and see if they can't just *like* you a whole lot."

Demry laughed again. So did the other people sitting around. And, seeing all of them, so did Acting Sergeant Shoemaker. Sitting in my upper bunk, I felt as though I were in a canoe floating down a river of inane chortling noise. I picked up the separated stock of my rifle and began to make paddling motions. Pausing for a moment, I let the stock trail as though I were steering. "My God, Celia," I said to Shoemaker. "Will these jungle noises never cease?"

Shoemaker stopped laughing, and gradually so did everyone else."

"I don't get you, Bonzo. You trying to be funny?"

"Yes," I said. I was sick of the lot of them. While Shoemaker pondered his rejoinder, I added, "Did you have something specific for me to do or were you just wasting time?"

"O.K., O.K.," he said. "Why don't you go on down to the mess hall and make yourself useful. Tell the mess sergeant I sent you."

It was a relief to get out of the barracks. I would gladly have volunteered for KP for the remaining eight days of basic. Among other things there was a feeling of grand accomplishment hovering about which I didn't like. It was self-indulgent. And it was false—the whole training period had been pretty much of a disappointment, in fact. We hadn't had any really stiff marches. There hadn't been any bayonet drill. Target shooting was mildly pleasurable, but there had been no more than two weeks of that—not enough time for real improvement. For what they might have been worth by way of aesthetic incentive, the formal aspects of the military remained unelaborated. Even the scenery was drab now that the illuminations of fall were over. A shoddy damp grayness penetrated everywhere, without the threat of a storm. All that was really happening here was time passing, steadily and unprofitably. But— and this was what excited them—certifiably.

Only eight days. And then fifteen days' leave at home before I was reassigned to a more reasonable environment. I gladly peeled potatoes in a corner of the kitchen. With any kind of solitary chore I could make the time trickle more nimbly. In every spiral shaving I cut loose I saw artful progress, as though I were freeing my own spirit from the crust of living in that place. By the time I splashed the last potato in the vat I felt miles away and much more at peace.

Calm is most regularly induced to enter the physical world by a series of ornamentations; it doesn't matter whether it is nature or oneself that executes them, so long as there is a stretch of repetitive exertion from a single source. Waves before the wind. The footfalls of a runner spinning the world beneath him. Paddle swirls in the wake of a canoe. Or curlicues of potato skin, as unbroken as the phrases sliding out from under the bowing hand of a cellist.

These repetitions are felt by our bodies, the deft, hardworking, and unsuspecting bundles in which we are enmeshed. Unsuspecting because it is by their efforts, the spasms of nerves and muscles that *we* command into rhythm, that they are calmed. And the calm rends them—plucks their fibers apart so that the spirit escapes to a dominant position. That is contentment, I suppose, and most people happen on it only by chance.

Since the complete exercise takes concentration as well as a certain amount of cunning, I was still exhilarated at my accomplished change in fortune as I served supper. This state of well-being even lasted until bedtime, although I knew that sleep would undo it. The Duc de Saint-Simon disliked the shock of a new day so much (I presume because his spirit was again stuck down in his body) that he would not leave his bed until his valet said to him, "Get up, get up, Monsieur le Duc, you have great things to do today!" How different Acting Sergeant Shoemaker's first words would be I did not care to imagine.

I waited until the latrine was empty and the lights were out in the squad bay before I went in to shave. I disliked rushing in the morning. As I stepped out of the latrine a blanket was thrown over my head. There was a great deal of shoving, and the noise of feet scraping on the floor. I was hit in the middle of the forehead. I gathered that a number of them were trying to beat me through the blanket, and they might have really done it had they used their fists, but, as I saw later, they were using the handles from the push brooms. There wasn't enough room to wield them effectively, and I heard a yelp when somebody holding the blanket over me was hit. I couldn't recognize their voices. In fact, they could have done without the bother of the blanket altogether—I doubt if I would have recognized their faces. After I recovered from the surprise, it took me very little time to break loose. I think I may have rammed one person into the drinking fountain. But as I was about to get rid of the blanket they gathered again and pushed me through the side door so swiftly that I fell heavily down the wooden steps. By the time I was on my feet again and clear of the blanket, they had scuttled back to their beds. I shook myself and padded back up the steps. I could have found them, I suppose, by their heavy breathing. The push broom handles—three of them—lay on the floor. I saw, too, that the blanket they had used was from my bed, so I had to go outdoors again to retrieve it. I folded it in half and shook the dust out of it. My hands were beginning to stiffen. They had received the few well-aimed strokes that had followed the initial one to my forehead.

I wanted to find it absurd, but my body took it as a humiliation. My forehead felt wet, although it wasn't bleeding. My hips hurt too, from the fall. But most of all, my stiff hands trembled, not in the fingers but from the wrist and elbow. I wanted to find the people absurd, but my fluttering arms and damp bruises took them seriously.

"Demry," I said, "where were you?"

He rolled onto his back to face me. "You're very big on waking me up, man. Last time I saw you, you were waking me up."

"You weren't scared, were you, Demry?"

"I was sleeping, man."

"You don't feel bad about it, do you?" I said.

"They didn't do you no real harm, did they?"

"No," I said. "But I hope you don't feel bad."

"Not me," he said. "I was catching up on my sleep."

I said, "Give me a boost up, would you, Demry? I'm somewhat stiff."

He thought about that awhile. But he was essentially a helpful fellow—even kind. He got out of bed and gave me a shove up as I clambered onto the upper bunk.

I lay on my side. I knew they were there. They had reached me, and it was I that was scuttling away. They had reached my state of mind—not with their blows but with their intentions. I was protected by my own strength, by the shortness of time, even by rules and laws—I had nothing to fear physically. But I had to scuttle away, because they tore apart the pleasant distance at which I lived.

All together they made a spirit that was opaque and probably at odds with itself, but very large and probing. The irony of it was that had I been small and weak, there would have been no need for them to gather. The irony of it was also that I had been fair. But irony would not work to keep the distance. They all at once came closer to me until what had been wandering creatures on my lawn became hands and faces pressed against the windows. All the time I'd thought I could cry "Whoosh!" and they would remove themselves like a carpet of pigeons from a park sidewalk. I had been taught, of course, to treat them better; I knew that fairness was not just a tactical consideration. What I had been taught and its manifestations, however, did not interest them; what did was my real state of mind. I think their final outburst was almost more curiosity than resentment. They probably wanted to see too.

Shoemaker came down the stairs from the cadre room, where he now lived. He shone his flashlight here and there about the room.

"All right, I want quiet," he said. The beam lighted on Ellridge kneeling on his lower bunk, his hands clutching the hollow bars that supported the upper.

"Aren't you going to get them?" Ellridge said to me.

"Shut up, Ellridge. You're on KP tomorrow," Shoemaker said. He shone the light on my face and approached. "Was it you, Bonzo?"

"Put out the light," I said.

"Was it you, Bonzo?"

I reached out and grabbed his throat. "Put out the light," I said. He did. "Be reasonable," I continued, shaking him just a little, "or I'll throttle you." I didn't mean it. He meant very little one way or the other. I let him go.

He retreated to the stairs and turned his light on, pointing it down. "You're on KP too, Bonzo."

I was glad that I hadn't hurt him. "All right," I said. That was reasonable of him.

I lay awake during the night. The moon was waxing again, and shining on the knob of the drinking fountain, but the air was still turbulent between the drinking fountain and me. Even though they slept, the turbulence stayed on. I didn't recognize those same cubic yards of air. Common pasturage during the day, they now kept on that way through the night. What had been mine now coincided with what was theirs at every corner. It was as though their gathered spirit could leave indelible traces.

The next day I was entirely present. They looked curiously at me as I served the meals—at the spot on my forehead, although they knew better than I where it came from. I was entirely present, as though they had thrown a blanket of my own skin over me and pulled it tight all the way to the ground.

MANDARINS

IN A

FARTHER FIELD

I 'VE LIVED IN WASHINGTON ALL MY LIFE except for going away summers and to college. Now I work here for Health, Education, and Welfare. In a report recommending me for promotion my boss said, "Mr. McEvoy is bright but not too bright." I got the promotion.

Before I became a dull bureaucrat, however, I was a spy. My death-defying mission was to attend the International Students' Festival at Helsinki one summer in the late fifties. I was at Yale, and some people who were in the same college with me got in touch with me. They were the local branch of the American Students' Union, which was sort of wishy-washy liberal, which was what I was, but they turned out to be in the pay of the government, which is what I turned out to be too. Anyway, they financed my trip over to the Students' Festival, where I was asked to talk it up with the Russian students and make reports on who seemed especially friendly. I assumed it was so that our people could get in touch with them and maybe proposition them. I didn't know for sure.

Of course, what happened was that the Russian students most eager to make friends were the ones who were supposed to find American students who were eager to make friends. Not too surprisingly, we found each other. By and large we were the only ones who could afford to buy drinks for anybody else. We were very popular at the local taverns—well-behaved, affluent, cheerful. I suppose we did something for the local tavern industry of brave little Finland. I got the impression they'd never had it so good, so it was foreign aid if nothing else.

On the tenth day, one of the friendly Russian students took me aside. At that time I still lingeringly thought I might make a contact, so I got quite excited. He said (he spoke pretty good English), "My friend, we are having a very good time."

"Yes," I said.

"I also," he said. "But I am not sure how we should say it in our reports."

"Our what?" I said. "Do you mean . . .?"

Looking at his face then, I lost a preconception. I'd thought that the Russians had been somewhat maligned in our popular press, but I'd believed the part that made them out to be pretty crude from the point of view of being cool. The Russian smiled. "Ah," he said, "I am a very bad man."

I couldn't help laughing.

"It doesn't matter," he said. "Let us simply continue."

"Or continue simply," I said. This took him a while to get, which was what I hoped, so he wouldn't have the better of me totally. Cheap and stupid of me.

We spent more and more time together, and he never brought the subject up again. We talked about Billie Holiday, Jack Teagarden, Sidney Bechet. I suppose that's the great cliché about Russian students now—that they are as enthusiastic about jazz musicians as grade school kids here are about baseball players. They have a crooning reverence in their voices as they go through a litany of the all-time greats.

My friend's name was Pavel. "Call me Paul," he said. I did until I figured out he didn't mean it. He took a sort of bearishly playful pleasure in adopting the clumsier manners of the Friendly Student Set.

All in all, we did have a very good time. The only Communist students who were nasty to me were the French. But they were nasty to Pavel too. They called him a bourgeois revolutionary, the "revolutionary" being ironically rather than historically intended. Oddly enough, I got mad on his behalf at that. I said I thought he was "the real thing," whether they or I liked it or not. It was one of those moments of vehement, loud naïveté that still make me twist with embarrassment. Fortunately Pavel persuaded me to leave before I'd really waded in and said a few words about how useless France was during World War II. I had planned, too, to make them feel puny by quoting the Russian war-casualty statistics on Pavel's behalf. When I told him all this right after we left the French, he pointed out that neither of us had much to do with those statistics.

"The only way to win arguments like that is to be dead," he said. "That is all that has a chance to impress them. And even that . . . As for your 'real thing,' the 'real thing' is not a person. The 'real thing' that you mean is a romance, the 'real thing' that they mean is a theory, and the 'real thing' I think of is a machine."

"No," I said, still aroused to a lofty pitch of loyalty to friends and therefore to all human beings. "People are much more important."

"Oh, I mean people," he said. "People like you and me."

But I was sure that besides being embarrassed by what I'd said to the French students, he'd also been touched that I'd been ready to go to bat for him. We went off and used some more of our expense accounts to buy drinks for ourselves and some Africans who turned up.

The summer passed. We said goodbye. I went back and finished college. I decided not to go right into law school. I decided I should work for one year at something that was indisputably good and got a job at H.E.W.

Three years later I was still there, even though I was, if not bored, at least physically restless. One day I sat down in the cafeteria in the basement of my office building, with my Salisbury steak and jello, and looked for the nine hundredth time at the Ben Shahn life-in-America murals. They're not bad—it's just that they weren't meant to be looked at nine hundred times. It was my own fault. I discovered I couldn't face another Salisbury steak and jello there. I went out for a walk.

I got as far as the huge concrete statues of heroic workhorses being controlled by huge concrete heroic workmen. They're right beside the Federal Trade Commission, across the street from the National Gallery. I tried to imagine the 1930s spirit that erected them. I was suspicious. My own devotion to service (I really do think H.E.W. is indisputably good) is so blue-button-down-collar and nine-to-five and progress-charts that I find it hard to conceive of the W.P.A. artist chipping away while his inner eye is on a personal vision of a new nation and a better world. Moreover, it would be sad to think that all he came up with was the concrete workhorses. And yet I find it sad, too, to think he was like me, just doing it because it was a job that was better than what most people were doing. That was my only claim to being in any way élite—that, in a high-school-civics-course frame of reference, I was a federal workhorse.

At that moment I saw Pavel. He'd seen me first. He looked very energetic and pleased. It struck him as very funny to come upon me, and he kept on grinning and pounding my shoulder. It took me until after we'd sorted out the details of how the two of us had ended up right there to feel as exuberant as he did.

He was working at the Soviet Embassy. He'd been there for some time. As cultural attaché and with some other duties. I told him what I was doing. I was surprisingly glad to see him too. We went off to have lunch at a seafood place.

"This is a very strange city," he said. "I have a very strange feeling that everyone will leave tomorrow. That everyone is here only for a moment. I can't believe that people are born here."

I felt I had a choice between two answers. One was that seventy-five percent of the population hadn't been born here. And other statistics. The other answer was that I had.

"It seems like Potemkin villages," he said. "Like Hollywood made it for making films. I can't find its core. However," he added, "I am not completely lost. There are details that are familiar, that are similar."

"Like what?"

"Those statues where we saw each other. They could be in a metro station in Russia. Except perhaps we would have machines in place of horses. But still—something crude and powerful. And the Indians in their—" He made a circle around his head with his finger.

"Turbans."

"—turbans, coming to get degrees in engineering, or asking for money, food, dams. I don't mean to condescend," he said. His English had got even better. "But they are similar, here and there," he went on. "And you and I are similar details."

"I don't know about that," I said, and told him about the report on me—"bright but not too bright."

"Oh, yes, yes," he said. "You can't imagine how similar."

That Saturday I took him on a tour of Washington. He was surprised to learn that I was born here and grew up here. "A real native."

It was always a daydream of mine to take an intelligent, appreciative foreigner on a tour of Washington. Pavel even wanted to see where I went to high school. In fact, he even wanted to hear detailed accounts of the football games I'd played in. It was nice. My ordinary childhood had never seemed so exotic to me.

We went to see the theater where Booth shot Lincoln. "Alexander II emancipated the serfs also and was assassinated also," he said. "But what is not similar in this case is, I think, that our nineteenth-century assassinations had more constructive significance."

That rattled me. "I think I see what you mean," I said. "I mean, if you're just being comparative."

He said he was just being comparative.

He was amazed to find a mosque in Washington, and he was amused that it was air-conditioned.

"Are there Muslims in America?"

I said I thought this mosque was mainly for diplomats. I

didn't want to go into the Black Muslims, because I didn't really know.

"There is a mosque in Leningrad," he said, "which is really for Soviet citizens, for people from the Central Asian republics."

I said I thought that the government was down on religion.

"That's not entirely true," he said, "but the mosque was built in the nineteenth century." I admired his answer. "You would like Russia," he said. "Would you ever be sent there?"

"With H.E.W.?" I said. "Are you kidding?"

"Oh," he said. "I thought you also worked with an overseas agency."

"That was just a summer thing," I said. "I was still in college."

I realized that I had at last given him a definite answer to his old question. I looked at him, but his face showed no satisfaction.

"You should take a trip if you can," he said. "You would like traveling in Russia."

"Are you still in intelligence work?"

"No," he said. "I work on consular matters—visas and other consular matters. I have also duties of cultural attaché."

His English got suddenly worse, as though he was trying to make the point that he hadn't understood the implications of my saying "Are you still?"

"But you would carry out intelligence assignments?" I said.

"How shall I say?" he said. "Our diplomatic and consular activity is governed by laws and conventions of proper diplomatic and consular activity."

"That's a very good answer," I said. His accent had got even thicker.

He smiled and put his palm on his chest. "I am a very good man," he said.

"The soothsayers of Rome used to smile when they passed each other on the street," I said.

He didn't understand. I explained.

"Oh, I see," he said. "You're very well read."
We continued the tour.

Every time I saw Pavel, I liked him more. And I felt I knew him better and better. Of course, I did think sometimes: He's still on the job, wants to find out state secrets. But then, I didn't know any, and I enjoyed his company.

I think he could see how I'd become the way I was better than I could see how he'd become the way he was. When we were talking about World War II, I discovered that he was a little older than me. I remembered that when the news came that the Japanese had surrendered, I'd just won a sailing race at summer camp. I was annoyed that no one noticed I'd won. He remembered the beginning of the war. He remembered being evacuated from Leningrad in a truck convoy. They drove across Lake Ladoga while Leningrad was being shelled from the other side. He lived on a farm until a year after the war was over, waiting for where they were moving back to to be built.

I wondered if all that made him different, tougher. He couldn't say; he didn't know how tough I was. In general, though, he thought Americans were cold-blooded. I said I thought that, on the contrary, they were mushy. He said that could be—they were cold-blooded about being mushy. He didn't mean to be insulting; he was just learning the language.

I wondered, too, what they had taught him in school. In my schools I was taught to be myself, to be a gentleman, to be a success. Several different things, it turned out. But what had they taught him in school?

Pavel worked harder at his embassy than I did at H.E.W., but I got to see him quite often. But there were still areas of misunderstanding—I'm not sure whose fault they were. For example, one time I decided to fix him up with the roommate of one of my girl friends. I confess I thought the girl I was interested in would be impressed. A real Russian. I was taking him along for his postcard value. I was guilty of that.

We were going over just for supper. The girls made a Mexican dinner and brought out some tequila. Pavel got smashed. Not sedate drunk, but just the way Hollywood/Broadway portrays Russians getting drunk. As soon as we got there he started putting it away. What the girls had in mind was a high-tone question-and-answer period. Pavel, ignoring a question about the preservation of folklore in rural Russia, leaned forward and said, "I look forward until fashions change in Leningrad and skirts are that short." The girls tucked their legs in and tugged their skirts down. "But what will I see there?" he said, turning to me. "Potatoes. Knees like potatoes. But here we have such sweet little knees, like little apples. Bright little apple knees." He got on his own knees and advanced toward the little apple knees, smacking his lips and sighing extravagantly. Both girls leaped from their chairs.

"I frighten you," he said. He turned to me. "I frighten them." To the girls again, as he continued to advance: "Come back, darling little apple knees, come back and I shall behave, my juicy little apples." He drooled. He caught it while it was still on his chin by damming it with his forefinger and flicking it back upside his lower lip. He lay down and laughed quietly to himself.

"I've got to go to work pretty early tomorrow," my girl friend said. "I've already been late twice this week."

It was only after several days that I decided the girls were too severe, especially in the context of how ordinary and uninterrupted our lives were.

I still had my suspicions about Pavel. He never mentioned that evening one way or the other, but one day he asked me if there were any corrupt officials where I worked. I gave him a fairly straight answer—that is, that the corruption was really petty, mainly to do with expense accounts and ducking out of hard jobs. When I asked him why he wanted to know, he said that he was just interested in making comparisons. He seemed to adhere to the convergence theory.

"In so many ways," he said, "we do not split the world in two. We are making it all the same. For better or for worse."

"Well," I said, "I hope for the better."

"That would be nice, of course," he said, "although you must know that you and I are not going to have any great effect."

I said, "If there are lots more people like us—"

"No," he said, "I don't mean people like us. I mean as single human beings, you and I. Neither you nor I have that desire, that high fever to devote each moment of our complete lives to changing all other lives."

I said that that might be so, but that I still worked pretty hard doing something that was pretty good.

"Of course," he said. "We aren't selfish. But we first of all wish to observe, to understand, to have our place in the world —and then we do our bit of good. We are officials, after all. But the real question is, who is leading the life we are building? We are not intending to sacrifice everything for the future. Therefore we keep trying to find pieces of this better life—like cooks who are tasting spoonful after spoonful of what they are preparing for others."

I laughed. I could see the people I knew in Washington tasting away: "Now there's a tasty program of a million dollars. I think we should take a little trip (*slurp*) just to see, and appoint a commission of a few of us, and run a little study (*slurp*) in our leisure time. . . ."

"It is not completely satisfying," Pavel said. "We are neither feasting nor starving. I don't mean riches or power that we nibble at. I mean possibilities of life in general. I mean time; I mean everything. We are not completing anything. And we are not being used up in order for anything to be complete. Every-one is becoming a little official. It is very badly arranged, I think. All the mechanics of policy should be only the outer defense for whatever part of life can go on. But the mechanics are still in the middle, taking up the space and the time, until no one knows anything else."

He paused again. I said I didn't think it worked out so badly. I was trying to get him to take it all less personally and not be so extreme.

"Were you ever ambitious?" he asked.

"Only a little," I said.

He laughed. "Only a little?" he said, and held his hands about six inches apart. "I was so ambitious at one time that I wanted things to melt in me. That is what I hoped for; that was my ambition precisely. To make many different things melt into one thing. I wanted to be able to announce something new. Perhaps to announce that *I* was something new."

"What?" I said.

"Oh," he said, "it was a very"—he held his hands out again and curled his fingers up—"a very nameless ambition."

"But that's not what you want now?"

"I am less ambitious now."

I think it was the next day I had my first visitor at work. I had just sent a note to Pavel (I knew it was awkward calling him at work) inviting him to go quail shooting at my uncle's farm in Virginia. My visitor took me to an empty conference room. He said, "There is no need for apprehension on your part; this is a routine check on all contacts of the nature of the contact you have been having with diplomatic personnel of one of a num-ber of specified foreign powers." He showed me his identifica-tion. "This identifies me to you, but let me encourage you to call this number"—he showed me a number—"to satisfy yourself that I am the agent identified on this identification."

I understood that he had to be thorough, but the third time through my very boring narration of every conversation Pavel and I ever had, I was beginning to lose patience. I, of course, wasn't supposed to say to anyone what I had been doing in Helsinki, but finally—just to get done—I let a long silence on the subject give a clue.

My visitor said, "Without going into the actual purposes of your visit to Helsinki, could you tell me if any other agency of our government was concerned?"

I looked uncomfortable and said nothing. From that silence he deduced that the whole thing was the concern of "another agency." At least he stopped asking questions, encouraged me again to call the phone number, and left.

The Friday before the Sunday Pavel and I were going to go quail shooting, I had a second visitor. He took me to the same empty conference room and showed me his identification. He was from another agency. Different phone number. He asked me if I would be kind enough to meet him that evening at an art gallery on M Street.

I went to the art gallery and the owner, after watching me awhile, asked my name. He took me to a back room. My visitor of that afternoon was there and said, "Hi. Sorry to put you out, but we're mildly curious about—"

"My social life."

He nodded.

"Are you worried about me or interested in him?" I asked.

"Oh," he said. "I guess you've had another visitor."

"I'm not supposed to say," I said.

"That's just routine, I suppose," he said reassuringly.

"I don't really see a possibility of anything you'd be interested in," I said. "Of course, I don't mean to presume on your expertise."

"I think you could do a little something for us," he said. "It wouldn't take any time, and we'll take care of any expenses. We don't want you to propose anything specific. It's not a question of that. Just find out what you can about whether he's interested in talking to someone a little further along the line. Always gently, discreetly, ambiguously. You know."

"No harm in that," I said. "But I really don't think there's anything there."

"Can you see him this weekend?"

"I'll try," I said. I could have said I'd arranged it already, but I wanted to impress him with my efficiency. I suppose that's one of my government habits. But having been a little dishonest, I made up for it by being frankly discouraging about the chances of my helping his project. I said, "You know what he was supposed to be up to in Helsinki?"

"Yes."

"Well, we reached a comfortable standoff on the whole subject."

"Let's just keep our eyes open for any counterindications on that score," he said.

We set up our next appointment. He gave me an *objet* to leave the gallery with. It was a nice-looking pewter inkstand. He said that I should bring it back next time. I was reassured by his agency's sense of economy.

Saturday morning I went to work for a half day. My boss called me in and said he thought I'd had my security check the year before. I said I had.

"I don't see why you're getting another," he said. "You're not thinking of leaving us for another job?"

I said no, that it was just some foreign contacts I had and that I hoped he wouldn't mention it.

He said of course, and that he'd said there was, of course, no question in his mind about my loyalty.

I said that was right.

He said that he'd said I didn't have any classified information available to me anyway.

I said that was right, except for one of the reports on school funds that had somehow got marked "Confidential."

"Oh, that," he said. "I don't know how that happened."

I felt better—I mean, I hadn't realized I'd been feeling bad until I felt better hearing us both dismiss it all. I was glad my boss sounded worried about my leaving. If you're going to be a workhorse, it's nice for people to know it.

On my way home that day, I went to have lunch at Bonat's with another H.E.W. fellow. It's not very far from the Soviet Embassy, so I wasn't too surprised when Pavel came in with a group of men all dressed in lumpy Russian suits. I began to get up. Pavel managed to get behind them and nod curtly to me. Then he turned away, his face blank and bored. It made me mad at him. It made me suspicious, or in any case righteous, about how open I was willing to be.

Sunday morning was a perfect gray fall day. Pavel and I left Washington for my uncle's farm at seven. Legal shooting began at eight.

The only reminder of what I was supposed to do was that Pavel asked how far away the farm was. I said about a thirty-five-mile drive.

"You see," he said, "we're only allowed to go fifty kilometers outside the city. That's about thirty miles."

"If you draw a straight line," I said, "the farm's only thirty miles away. The drive is sort of roundabout."

We drove past the new C.I.A. building in Langley. He didn't look up.

We picked up the tenant farmer's dog, a middle-aged black Labrador, and got the guns from the main house. The dog began to jump when he saw the guns. He knew I was a terrible shot, but he may have had hopes for the other fellow. He kept nudging Pavel's knee with his nose.

An odd thing happened about then. I know it may seem paradoxical, but hunting was the most pastoral, quiet, private, and gentle part of my life. My uncle got the farm when I was nine. It wasn't in the gentleman-farmer Middleburg-Warrenton axis. It was north of all that, in an untidy backwater of independent beef and dairy farms. For example, there were more likely to be pigs than horses in the back yard, and there was a lot of rocky, weedy wasteland. More barbed wire than rail fence. More tar paper and corrugated metal than wood in the sheds, barns, and silos. So when I was going to school I only brought friends out whom I really trusted to like doing nothing and who would understand what was nice about the place being unimproved, dreary, and still. Later on I preferred going alone—especially when hunting. And later yet I never gave any thought to the condition of the country as far as the Health, Education, or Welfare went. I'd brought no visitors or thoughts there since I was sixteen. So, although I'd taken Pavel around Washington and hadn't minded introducing him to girls I knew, just before we set out with the dog to go through a stretch of woods I felt a resentment at his intrusion. His intrusion into my land, into a piece of nurtured schizophrenia that gave my ordinary life its only other dimension. I felt more secretive about the feelings I had out there than any I had in the institutions I went to or worked for. I was even secretive about keeping my feelings secret.

We set off through the woods, each of us with a double-barreled 20-gauge shotgun, the dog trotting in and out of the oak trees and sniffing deeply at the piles of leaves by the roots. Before we got out of the woods, Pavel stopped me and asked how big a quail was. I showed him with my hands. What shape? I drew a picture in some mud with a stick. I thought I'd better tell him how they'd go up when the dog ran into a covey.

"Yes," he said, "we have quail too. *Perepyolka.*"

"Did you do a lot of hunting?" I asked. It struck me that the only picture of Russian hunting I could imagine was a Turgenev/Tolstoy one.

"Yes," he said. "Not for quail so much as for—I don't know the name. *Kurapatka.*" He drew a picture in the mud.

"Some kind of grouse?" I said. "Or partridge."

"And this," he said. He drew another picture.

"It's either a woodcock or a snipe," I said. "That's sort of in between."

"Smaller," he said. "*Byeskaz.*"

"Snipe."

"And ducks," he said. "They fly down the rivers in the fall. They fly all the way to Persia. Even to India, they say."

We stepped out of the woods. The meadow stretched for more than a mile, rolling down to another stretch of woods that lined a creek. The grass was knee high in places. There were a few solitary stunted pines, some flowering thistles, and dried-out Queen Anne's lace. High above us there was a wind blowing the clouds slowly to the west, where—far in the distance—we could see the Blue Ridge. There the sun was shining through breaks in the cloud cover.

He walked ahead of me and stopped to look. I felt a twist of annoyance. The dog trotted stiffly back to him and nudged his knee. Pavel didn't pay any attention to him and the dog lay down heavily, raising his eyes to me to see if I'd be any quicker to get down to hunting. Pavel turned around and looked at me curiously. I don't know what he saw in my face—I was in the middle of changing my mind about having him there. After all, he was as much another dimension as the place. He raised his free arm and let it fall back to his side.

He said, "I would never have known this part of the world was like this."

The dog got up, stretched, and yawned. I said to him, "Hie on." He began to quarter the field with his stiff trot, going back and forth like a windshield wiper, always about thirty yards in front of us. We went across the field, pulling our legs through the tall grass, the dog padding back and forth, concentrated and happy, and far, far in front of us the Blue Ridge were spotted with moving sun and shadow.

The day went by as though it were tied to us—slowly when we were going slowly through the grass, enveloped and calmed by the still air; and then whirring up with the covey, swinging with the guns, bounding around with the dog as he eddied through the cover finding the fallen birds; and then stopping with long bright surprise as a single quail popped up and away past our empty guns; and settling on us again as we passed through some more woods and into a farther field.

We circled back to the house about four in the afternoon. Seven quail. Not bad, not good. We thought it was a triumph, and the dog thought we were geniuses, since he couldn't count. We cleaned the birds and fed him the hearts and livers. We fried two of the birds, along with some bacon. We made a fire and let the dog come in the house. We had a few drinks and watched the sun go down.

Just as we were getting back into the car after dropping the dog off at the tenant farmer's house, I was feeling so full and effusive that I almost told him everything about what I was supposed to ask him. As a kind of present of confidence. Of course, I checked myself.

In fact, I could almost feel the caution—the security—fence off that whole subject in my mind. It was a sudden shock, as though something clanged down around me. At first I was pleased that I knew how to keep quiet even after a few drinks. Then I had a sense of resentment even stronger than I'd had in the morning at Pavel for coming into my land. But it was a more frustrated resentment, because there was nothing I really wanted to do about this intrusion. In a way, it was my own.

The following Tuesday I went back to the art gallery on M Street. I was careful to bring back the *objet.* I went to the back room and said, "No go."

My visitor from the other agency said, "What did he say?"

I said, "He's very loyal, that's all." For some reason I'd thought that would be all I'd have to say.

"How do you know?"

"He said so," I said. "Sort of." I wasn't very well prepared. It upset me, because I usually like to do presentations well— especially to other agencies.

"What *did* he say?"

"He didn't say it in so many words," I said. "I just inferred that he liked it here O.K., but that he would be glad to get back. That's all."

"How do you know?"

And so it went. Did Pavel try to make an overture to me? Did he complain about any of his superiors? Did he seem very knowledgeable about the United States? Did he have any special interests? (I said he liked hunting.) What did he say about girl friends? Did he express himself in any way about his job? Was he overworked? Underworked? Bored? Tired? Did he need money? Et cetera. We went over the same ground several times, each time with different footwork.

"I guess it's a blind alley," I said at last.

"That seems to be your unshakable opinion," the man said. He was annoyed. "Did it occur to you that you may have done a disservice to your friend as well as to us by not really pursuing the matter as we agreed?"

"Of course," I said.

We sat in silence for a while. I thought he was trying to think up some new way to get at me, but finally he just asked what my expenses had come to. I said I'd skip the expenses.

"I'd just as soon you didn't," he said. "It makes the record sloppy. How far did you drive?"

"Seventy miles or so," I said. "Round trip."

"Beyond the thirty-mile limit?" he said.

"No," I said, and explained. He shrugged and counted out

some cash for the driving expenses. He said he'd be in touch if necessary.

During the next day I didn't think too much about it all. I thought I'd adroitly made myself as neutral as possible over something that could be forgotten.

The day after that I had a sudden fit of thinking I'd been wrong. Maybe the man was right. Maybe he knew much more than I did about Pavel's wanting to come over and I was the only way to contact Pavel, but he couldn't trust me with the whole story.

But then I thought Pavel would surely have spoken to me. He knew me; he was a friend of mine. Of course, institutions, I thought, even in this country, know more than friends. I had a friend at Yale, a graduate student, whose girl friend found out he was going to propose to her when she saw, by chance, his application for renewal of his research grant. He'd asked for more money, and explained to the foundation that he was going to get married. She said nothing. When he got the money he asked her to marry him. She wasn't mad that the foundation knew before she did. She knew that that's how life is nowadays.

I balanced all these thoughts by thinking I'd been deceitful with Pavel, that one of the few values I still imagined myself holding had to do with friendship, with being truthful in friendship. I realized that I hadn't ever been put in a position where I had to examine what I meant by friendship. All I'd ever had to do was put a drunk to bed, vote for a friend's membership in a club, go to weddings. I hadn't even had to lend anyone more than twenty dollars.

The third day, I decided that on the basis of the past week my life was gray and feeble. I realized I should have resolved to play it out all the way. I became obsessed with garish, disruptive possibilities. No matter which way Pavel was working, I should have hired a girl to seduce him, offered him stock in General Motors, a plane ticket to Rio. Asked him to rob a bank. Anything to see in his face what was in his mind. I wanted to find out things just for myself. To have some interest—even some duplicity—of my own.

Even when I subsided and was working quietly along on my H.E.W. chores, I would suddenly think that at the very least I should have asked Pavel to confide in me—offered to explain my own small part—exchanged my own fabulous lies for his fabulous lies, some invention of what I was for his invention of what he was. At least that—at the very, very least.

But I subsided even further. I began to guess that the only value at the bottom of my life was preservation of a personal status quo. Me in my right place. I was apparently ready to work for twenty years—or, as they used to say around the office, work for one year twenty times.

But after a week of yearning for turbulence and revelation, the automatic pilot of my life kept me routine. It took a special effort to lift the phone and call Pavel at home. I was even relieved when there was no answer. But I kept calling regularly until I had worked up enough frustration to call the Soviet Embassy the next day. They said he wasn't in—to try the consular affairs number. I did. They said there to call the embassy number. I did. They asked me to leave my name and number and said he would call when available. He didn't. I called again the next day. Same runaround. I went to his apartment. No one home. I left a note. Next day still no response. I had my secretary dial the embassy number while I dialed the consular affairs number. They both said to call the other number. I said to the embassy that I was connected to the consular number and that the consular people said to call them. There was a silence. Then they gave a third number. I called that. A man answered and said to call the other two numbers.

"No," I said. "I've just called them."

Silence. "Who do you wish?" I told him again. Silence. Then a conversation aside in Russian. The man said, "Not available."

"Oh, well," I said, "I'll leave a message."

"Not available," the man said. "Not available on a permanent basis."

"What does *that* mean?" I said, but he hung up.

For a moment I assumed that it meant something dire. I couldn't think of anything to do, of course. I didn't know how to get hold of my contact from the other agency. What could he do anyway? Raid the Soviet Embassy?

My secretary went out for lunch. I stayed at my desk thinking. I kept lapsing away from the problem into all my other thoughts—thoughts about what my yearning for disruption meant to me or about me. I began to feel that my mind had suddenly become double-jointed. I began to have a yearning for the boring competence I'd developed over the past three years, and then, like the coils of a Slinky toy going down a flight of stairs, my thoughts would flip over and be about how to cut loose from it all.

Pavel came into the office. "Farewell, farewell," he said, "unless you haven't had lunch yet."

"I thought you were supposed to be in trouble," I said.

"Ah," he said. "What have you been doing?"

"I've been trying to call you."

"You were worried about me?" he asked.

"Of course I was."

"Then you are not yet completely dead as a human being," he said.

"What's going on? What are you doing? Where are you going?"

"To Paris," he said. "Don't you think that's nice?"

"I thought you'd done something bad," I said.

"Perhaps I have," he said, "and Paris is my reward."

"Be serious," I said. "I wish you'd tell me exactly what's going on."

"Come have lunch," Pavel said. "I want to eat a crab before I leave."

We took a cab up to a restaurant by the National Theater and had crabs.

"This is a perfectly normal move, then," I said. "You're just getting on in the world."

"Yes," he said. "This is still all my career."

"I didn't mean just that," I said. "I thought you'd gotten mixed up in something important. I mean, what were you doing here, really?"

"I'm surprised that you still want to know the mechanics of things," he said. "I mean for yourself. You would be bored. Truthfully. The mechanics of things are a bad novel you read when you cannot sleep. You do not want to remember them and you spend time thinking about them anyway. That is really all you should know about that. Now let me tell you something else."

I didn't know about all that. I said that if he were to tell me anything he didn't want me to talk about, he could be sure I would keep a promise to him just as well as any promises I made to institutions. I said I just wanted to know about him.

"It would give me great satisfaction to build a city," he said, ignoring what I had just said. "Or to grow a forest. But I will not. Nor you. We are enmeshed. The most exalted feelings we will have will be on the day of marriage, of the birth of a child, of a peaceful time. That small fraction of our lives will be the only time our bodies will be full of blood and alive. The rest of the time is for mechanics—and bad jokes about how dull we are. We are not artists or leaders. When I was young I wanted to be as triumphant and right as Lenin. Then—a little older—I wanted every moment of my life to be as full and right, in another way, as when I first began to see paintings in museums. I thought I could feel life at all times as though it were painted by Cranach, Rembrandt, Matisse. But afterward I saw that of my life, that is the smallest fraction of all. Triumph and rightness—whether of Lenin or Matisse—are not possible. They are not my possibility. And that is why I am content to cultivate these small fractions of life that mean something to me. It is not possible to find the whole. Why? I will tell you. Ever since men learned to throw stones, most of us have been at a distance from the rest of life. There are very few who can do anything but keep backing away with their stones. That is why I am content with the fractions of time when that is not so. For example, the day at your farm was a fraction about which I am very satisfied. And yet *you* still wish to know everything, because you still believe that life is not fractions, that people are not fractions to each other. I will tell you—no matter what I would explain to you, you will not know more than a fraction. Isn't that right? You know that I am right."

I said I didn't know.

"Well, it isn't something to complain about," he said. "I am not complaining. I just came to say goodbye. One would-be mandarin to another."

We left the restaurant and walked until he found a cab.

"Maybe I'll be able to come see you in Paris," I said.

"That would be nice, of course," he said.

He went off in the cab, and I walked down Pennsylvania Avenue past the Justice Department. It was true that I had been sure, in a prosaic way, that knowing more about anything or anyone, I would be able to embrace more, unite more in myself, and blend my virtues and accomplishments into a whole that was in turn part of a larger whole of everyone's virtues and accomplishments. I had assumed that the proper arranging of things in the world was something that I could become a part of to the point where everything that went right, that was brought into its place, would give me satisfaction.

That is what I thought it was to be a mandarin. That was

not what Pavel meant. What he meant was resignation to fractions—resignation to having to maneuver his life through what was unavoidably being done; resignation to rationing his pleasures, to restricting them to such bland and inert sharers as me; to admitting that, of the part of life that could still go on, these fractions were all he would ever loose his natural feelings toward.

As for myself, in several ways I had divided the world into compatible, even mutually attractive, halves. Theirs and ours, to name just one set. Or the urge to be spontaneous and disruptive and free (without personal consequences) and the satisfaction of being an agent of benefit (without inflicting anything that anyone could say was not good).

I'd always had a balanced view. I'd always felt I could be within reach of both halves of everything.

But by the time I got to the horses on the Capitol side of the Federal Trade Commission I was giving in. I think I had been planning to walk by them because I'd run into Pavel there, and also because they stood for all the convergences I'd expected in my own life or in the way the world was meant to go. I had even worked out such elaborate similes as the likeness of the way I'd hoped to see with how a horse sees, an eye on each side. But when I got there, all this conscious and optimistic symbolism gave way. It was all in pieces. I remembered thinking that, as a last comfort, as a last justification, I had always been able to think of myself as a federal workhorse. That had been sweetly imaginary.

I'd thought my ambitions were safe because they were so orthodox and modest. But those notions of duty, labor, and what couldn't be called anything but good weren't really the ambitions of a person. And as for personal ambitions, I really hadn't even hoped for as much as Pavel had. And there we were, both settled in. Not even as workhorses. We were less like horses than like the flies that follow them. Bottle-green mandarin flies following the federal horses, who aren't people, after all. And we could stare with flies' multiple-prism eyes at all that might be going on or not, but what we ended up seeing for ourselves was fractions, repeated and repeated, from which we could subtract the few that made up our small personal lives.

CONNAISSANCE

DES ARTS

MISS HOGENTOGLER WAS A WAITRESS at the Huddle, where I ate a late breakfast after composition class, before I went to my drama class at noon. We had a half hour alone three days a week.

At first I told Miss Hogentogler all the clever things I'd heard when I was in college. She was enchanted by the East— by the East she meant Boston and New York. She wished to be thin, beautiful, and wicked. Later that year she did become beautiful.

She had fine brown hair, a high broad forehead, a large mouth, but with enough bone in her chin and cheeks to carry it off. But it was wishing that changed her. Or perhaps she was always beautiful and I finally saw it.

During the fall I thought she was foolish and cute. She loved to have long talks. She prepared for them—but not in order to dominate them. Toward the end she would droop with submissive yearning: "Oh, Mr. Hendricks, I had no idea it was so complicated."

Miss Hogentogler loved to hear stories of elegant meanness, stories in which people's feelings were crushed by a single word. I quickly ran through the famous lines: Whistler to Oscar Wilde; George Bernard Shaw about his American publisher; John Wilkes's famous zeugma (Mr. Interlocutor to Mr. Wilkes: You, sir, will die either on the gallows or of a horrible venereal disease. Mr. Wilkes: That depends, sir, on whether I embrace your political principles—or your mistress). I think I remembered some Rochefoucauld and some Voltaire.

I tried a few jokes of my own. She laughed politely. She had a beautiful polite laugh—as she sensed a punch line coming she would store up her polite laugh behind her large white teeth and then slowly unbite it.

I told her that on a poem of mine that I had submitted to a poet-teacher I admired, she had written, "A gracefully minted coin—of small denomination."

Honorée opened her teeth. "Oh, that's *wonderful!*"

I tried to think of *bons mots* of which I had not been the butt. A friend of mine—at least someone I knew—said of Mary McCarthy's oeuvre, "All her *romans* have feet of *clé*." I had to explain this to Honorée, while she wrote it down on a napkin.

I told her that I'd heard someone say (I knew someone who'd heard someone say) *à propos* of a philosophy grad student who stayed married to a shrew because she was typing his thesis, "That's putting Descartes before divorce."

"Oh, Mr. Hendricks," Honorée said, "did you really hear that?"

I said, "Yes."

"Well, tell me, Mr. Hendricks, was this because—I mean, tell me honestly—is this because it was just men talking to each other? Are men wittier than women?"

"No, I don't think so."

"Are you sure?"

"Yes."

"Was the person who said this in college or graduate school? I mean, did they get that way by trying? Can you get that way by trying?"

I cleared my throat. I said, "Don't you think, Miss Hogentogler, that the phrase 'natural sophistication' is suspect? And in any event this sort of thing isn't of the essence. Why are you so concerned about . . ."

"Oh, Mr. Hendricks, I don't *know* why."

It was a silly question on my part. An unfair question. I knew she had a crush on me. I was lonely. I was still finishing my thesis and worked long hours—not hard, but long. Something about me irritated my new colleagues. I had the coiled shyness of an only child who had gone to a large boarding school and a large university and who had learned to observe critically at a very early age. If others observed me as I observed them, I had every reason to be wary.

I was born of handsome parents who lived a careful—or do

I mean carefree?—life and who didn't discover I was very little trouble until I was thirteen. At that point—during vacations—there came a sudden vault into grown-up worlds. My mother said to her cousin Josie (a woman I adored), "You know, Oliver's manners are so good I can take him anywhere."

When I was fourteen this cousin took me out to lunch. She was a beautiful woman—or at least glamorous in the style that was then just passing: large shiny lips framed in rouged cheeks and a massive set of hair, broad shoulders swaggering with fur. She was as impressive as a ship entering a small harbor.

I choose that simile for a reason. My first effort to entertain this magnificent woman was this: Why is the *Queen Mary* coming into dock like a woman getting into her girdle? Answer: Because it takes a lot of little tugs.

Cousin Josie laughed politely. She said, "Well, I certainly hope you didn't have me in mind."

I blushed. It was a childish joke. I struggled to get to the surface of my feelings. I often had the sensation of drowning in a turbulent river of my feelings in her presence. In fact, her presence and my feelings were one fast-flowing confusion.

I said I didn't imagine she wore a girdle.

She laughed. I sensed her small ripple of pleasure. It engulfed me.

I popped back up to say that there was something she could tell me that I was curious about: what did it really *feel* like to be a beautiful woman?

She laughed again, but she was pleased on a larger scale. I was ready and dog-paddled to the crest of this wave.

She said, "Well, that's awfully sweet . . . but it's a hard question. It reminds me—a friend of mine asked me once what it was like to kiss a man with a mustache."

The thought of cousin Josie kissing a man with or without a mustache submerged me again.

She said, "I told her it was like eating an oyster with a toothbrush. Oh, dear—I shouldn't have said that. Oh, well."

I didn't get it. Kissing was still a mystery to me. I thought, for some reason, that you sucked your lips dry before applying them.

Later on during lunch I told Josie she reminded me of Fabrizio's aunt in *The Charterhouse of Parma*. She hadn't read it, so I had the pleasure of telling her the plot. I turned it to fit what I took to be the facts of our case even more snugly.

Although cousin Josie was considered by my parents to be racy (she was divorced and talked about men and women a lot), she was in fact a conventional woman. She remarried when I was sixteen, after the fever of my affections had peaked. I had carried a torch for her for more than a year and a half. During that time I wrote poems to her, one of which I finally mailed. By that time I had learned a complete version of the facts of life—second-hand, to be sure, but I think they struck a richer chord than any possible first-hand encounter might have. But what I had learned at fifteen and a half was enough to push some of the poems I wrote from the ethereal to the erotic.

At Thanksgiving, cousin Josie took me aside for a talk. We went to the library and she closed the door. She half sat on my father's desk. She asked how I liked school. I felt that for the first time I might have the upper hand. It was a wonderful nervous sensation. Josie finally took the poem out of her pocketbook. The plot was not entirely original—a young man falls in love with the statue of a goddess, who comes to life and loves him for his love which brought her to life.

Josie put on her glasses to read. Watching the stems slither under her hair, finding their way between the top of her ear and her scalp, was a light sea I took well.

Josie looked up and said, "You know, I showed this to a friend of mine who knows a lot about poetry and he said that you have a lot of talent—he was amazed when I told him you're only fifteen."

I said, "I didn't think you'd show it to your friends."

She said, "Well, I was a little worried about it. You see, I may have been a little dumb. I'm afraid I may not have understood. This may sound awfully silly . . . you see, I've always been just as fond of you as I could be."

I turned away and paced impatiently. It was a gesture only; I still didn't know what was bound to come.

Josie said, "I may be wrong, but it seems to me now you may be trying out your feelings—I remember very well how strong and confusing these growing-up feelings can be—and I certainly don't want to hurt your feelings, but I don't want you to be hurt by your own feelings either. And I'm afraid that they may have been getting . . ." She squeezed her lips together and turned the palm of one hand up.

I interrupted. "I'm not 'trying out' feelings. I'm writing about—"

Josie said, "Well, yes. But when you write this—it's really very good, you know—when you write this:

> *'His fingertips that brush the pale marmoreal skin*
> *Burn suddenly with fleshly fire*
> *And change the touch that had been dreaded sin*
> *To higher right and better law—Desire!'*

Well, all I can think is that it wouldn't really be like that in real life—"

"It would," I said. "It would because—"

"Oliver," she said, cautioning me.

"It's you!" I said.

I felt that this revelation would undo her. I had seen her nerves. But behind her nerves she was horribly self-possessed. I realized a little later that she'd been prepared for any declaration I had the power to make.

She said, "I know you're so sweet that I just can't be cross. But you really shouldn't let yourself get carried away. . . ."

While she was talking I considered what else I could do. I had another poem, but that was out. It went further in some ways—it was a shipwreck poem, in which only two reach a desert shore. I also knew that now I was much less interested in long-term love—I had come to see several flaws in her in the last minute—but I was all the more interested in a real kiss.

Josie said, "Real feelings are much more complicated—the feelings a woman has for a man have to do with so many more emotions. . . . There has to be more or there really just isn't real feeling at all."

That was certainly the catechism of the fifties. I believed it. I believed she believed it and that she was right to believe it. In fact, the most complicated parts of my imagining were not the physical setting (loose togas, storm-tattered skirt, etc.); they were rather the array of other emotions I devised for her to feel for me: gratitude, pity, amusement, curiosity—even family loyalty. I always imagined at least a half dozen concurrent feelings to shore up the plausibility of her one giddy spark of dangerous affection. So I was irritated when she told *me*: "Real feelings are much more complicated."

Irritated, but helpless. Because while she'd been talking I'd had to admit to myself that I didn't have the courage to try to kiss her. I was as tall as she was, but I was thin and I had the terrible feeling that she was stronger than I was.

It had also crossed my mind to tell her either that I was so miserable that I was going to leave school for good or that one of the masters had tried to seduce me and that I was in desperate need of reassurance. I wasn't sure why I couldn't try these tacks; I just knew I couldn't.

I said, "Give me back the poem."

She handed it to me and I tore it up.

She said, "Oh, Ollie."

I said, "Don't call me that."

She pushed herself up from the desk. Our eyes were on the same level. I suddenly began to move toward her, some small wish in me suddenly swimming hard, leaping and plunging upstream into her look. But there was no real force in the rest of me; I was just weakly staggering. She put her arms out. I took another dizzy step, my eyes blindly on hers. She caught me by the shoulders and held me at arms' length.

Then I realized she was looking at me with pleasure—a mild, completely controlled pleasure.

She said, "You really are so sweet. What am I going to do with you? Believe me, if I were a girl your age I really don't know what—" She squeezed my shoulders, picked up her pocketbook, and left. I don't believe she knew exactly what she was doing, but she had done it neatly. When she left I didn't have any feeling left at all, not one bit.

When I told Honorée this story I left out that last part—I think I thought she wouldn't understand. But I was prepared for her to be stabbed by the poignancy. Instead she was filled with admiration for cousin Josie. Miss Hogentogler chose to regard my adolescent anguish as an anecdotal frame for the portrait of an elegant lady. And yet it was Miss Hogentogler who was by far my best student in our section of composition and rhetoric.

I found that I looked forward to correcting my students' papers. I divided the themes by sex and saved the girls' for last. It was the most erotic experience of the week. When I would write a comment in the margin—"You can do better than *this*, Miss Akerblad"—the very act of adding the name would arouse me as though I had surreptitiously touched her. And the thought of her writing out corrections at my command made it seem as though she were shyly acquiescing. I would pore over the paper again and feverishly write out, at elaborate length, alternate ways for her to correct the dangling modifier, comma splice, or missing antecedent.

Among the choices of titles that the department assigned for the first freshman theme was "My Life Story."

"My name is Honorée Hogentogler," she wrote. "Honorée means honored in French. However my family name is of German racial origin. My sister's name is Desirée. That means desired in French also. The other names in our family are normal. However our dog is named Kartoffel. This means potato in the German language. He is called that because of his supposed predilection for such a vegetable." And so it went to the end, listing the events and honors of her life in stiff, nervous sentences. Wapsi Valley High girls' gymnastics team. Choral group. Bell lyre in the marching band. Valedictorian. In short, whole-apple goodness. What interested me more was that when I said to her, "Instead of 'because of his supposed predilection for such a vegetable,' why don't you say 'because he likes potatoes'?" she replied, "I was being funny."

I knew she was not telling the truth. This slight taint attracted me.

At this point I discovered why some of my colleagues didn't like me. It was the way I dressed. The very style that so pleased Miss Hogentogler offended them. My officemate wore cowboy clothes. It was he who told me that several people had mentioned that they thought I was deliberately dressing up to put them down. Although they wore cowboy clothes, some of them came from back East, though not Miss Hogentogler's East. One of them came from Fitchburg, Massachusetts. But even he had surely encountered a coat and tie at some time.

They wished their students to call them by their first names, and this wish was somehow connected to their cowboy clothes —their theory being that their manner would help bridge the gap between their own rigorous intellects and those of their students, and at the same time align them with their students in a comforting way against the difficult fopperies of, say, Jane Austen. Insofar as they applied this theory to themselves, it was fine with me. But as they extended it to me, I became an illustration of conspicuous consumption—somehow a striped shirt with a white collar was a finger in the eye of democracy. My reaction to my officemate's advice was to get my three-piece suit out of mothballs. The vest had small notched lapels; the tweed itself was green with squares drawn in bright orange lines—a borderline case between a country squire going bird shooting and a Newmarket tout. My officemate unfortunately was sick the next day, but this suit had a strong effect on Miss Hogentogler. The day after I wore it she told me she'd dreamed of it. In her dream it, and she and I, went to Europe together.

"What was funny," she said, "was that we went by train. Of course, maybe the train got put on a boat. Did you ever go by boat?"

I said, "Only once by ship. Otherwise by plane."

She said, "Well, in my dream it couldn't have been by plane. I'm terrified of planes. I've had dreams of planes crashing. I'm in my room at home—it's on the top floor and there are all these planes flying around. Then one of them begins to fall right toward the house, right toward my room, and then it comes right through the ceiling right on top of me."

I said, "This plane isn't firing a gun from its nose, is it?"

"No," she said. "It's just an ordinary plane."

"Miss Hogentogler, have you ever read any Freud?"

She said, "I don't *think* so."

I said, "Have you ever slept with anyone?"

She laughed and looked out the window. Then she looked at my face, her gaze focusing on one of my eyes and then the other. Which eye had the right answer?

"Almost," she said.

"Almost?"

"It was really very funny," she said. "It was really just very amusing."

I told her about Freud. It occurred to me as I spoke that I had initially acquired Freud through oral tradition too. But Miss Hogentogler believed every word I said.

Public speaking was part of rhetoric and composition. One of the assigned topics from English HQ was "My Favorite Magazine."

Honorée, when her turn came, said, "This assignment
is one that finally awakened my interest. I at last have a speech
topic that is nearly as interesting as 'My Summer Job.' My
favorite magazine is of course *Hot Rod.*" She held it up daintily
between her thumb and forefinger. She'd painted her short nails
bright pink for the occasion. "I love to get up at the crack of
dawn and get right to work on *Hot Rod*'s latest idea—how to
put a full race cam on your family station wagon. *Hot Rod* is
full of brilliant writing which evokes all my favorite smells—be
they burning rubber from laying a strip or hot exhaust from the
muffler by-pass. Although I have to say the prose is not as good
as my favorite book, which is the repair manual for a fifty-two
Ford."

Her irony grew heavier, and the class began to laugh.

My own thoughts were suddenly possessive: Why was she
playing to the boys? Miss Quist and Miss O'Rourke weren't
laughing. Did she want these boys to like her, after all? Moreover, she was making them laugh in a way that made me the
butt—as though I were responsible for the speech topics, as
though this class were capable of anything more. I looked
down at Honorée's speech-grading blank. Section 4 was Eye
Contact. I circled Poor, then changed it to Fair. I thought she'd
better keep in mind to whom she should address herself. But I
rated the speech excellent as a whole. In all the other blanks
except Voice I circled Excellent. I looked up and saw Honorée
smiling at me tentatively, her face now oddly pale after the
flush of victory at her first laugh. I wrote in the margin, "You
have a beautiful voice, Miss Hogentogler," and as though I
were alone in my office, I felt the erotic power of marginal
comment.

The next speaker gave me his grading blank and went to
the lectern. He was a tall conscientious boy with a blond crew
cut that looked as though it had been stuck in quill by quill at
the peak of the long flat slope of his forehead. He stood in
silence for a moment. I said, "Go right ahead."

He said, "My favorite magazine is *Hot Rod.*"

Laughter. Honorée flushed with triumph again.

I said, "That's all right. I'm sure Miss Hogentogler has left room for some genuine appreciation of the subject." Honorée beamed at me across the room.

Honorée said to me that since she knew my thesis topic was Elizabethan drama, she would like to ask me some questions about drama. I said fine. She said, "Do you think I could be an actress?"

I said, "Not on the Elizabethan stage."

She looked puzzled.

I said, "The girls' parts were played by boys."

She said, "Oh, Mr. Hendricks. Don't be droll."

I said, "Why this sudden interest?"

"It's not sudden. I had the female lead in our high school play. I played Eliza Doolittle in *My Fair Lady.*"

I said, "How did you manage the accents?"

She said, "Well, we mostly concentrated on the music, but I can do a sort of English accent. Anyway, I was thinking of taking an acting class, but I was worried about . . ."

"About?"

"Well . . . how I look."

She took a step back so that I could see her full-length over the lunch counter. She stood completely still, inviting inspection. I felt a peculiar emotion—a harsh peppermint thrill.

I said, "Well, that uniform isn't the most flattering thing."

Honorée's face burned. Her lips parted slightly and then stayed completely still. I looked down and was suddenly touched by her small plump feet squeezed into her tennis shoes.

I said, "You have wonderful coloring. And you look healthy—health is a large part of good looks."

I wished to give her more than this modest compliment, but

I babbled on. "It occurs to me you *could* do more. Your hair is too fine to wear that long. You should get it cut."

Her gaze was steady.

I said, "I don't know much about make-up so I can't say with certainty, but you should give up the lip gloss. I think lip gloss is for cute little Cupid's bows. Your mouth is too full for . . . But don't go to dark lipstick. What's wrong with pink? A nice tea-rose pink. And then simplify your clothes—the ones you wear to class are far too busy."

Honorée said softly, "I guess I ought to lose some weight."

I said with a donnish chuckle, "Not from your lips." Honorée didn't laugh. I said, "No, no. Not much. When you simplify everything you may find you won't have to. Take your hands." Honorée put her hands flat on the counter, palms down.

I said, "You shouldn't bite your nails. It makes your hands look fat."

Honorée's fingers curl up, but she wills them open again.

I know I've gone too far, but we are both silent, watching her hands on the counter.

I finally said, "Actually, your hands are very well shaped, broad handsome hands."

Honorée said, "I'll do what you say. I'll do just what you say."

On the other side of the statue *Pioneer Woman,* two girls sat down to eat their lunch. They began to discuss the student evaluation forms they had filled in.

"You have Matthews in psych, don't you? What'd you give him?"

"Are you kidding? I let him have it. Of course, I'm pulling a D, so they won't count it as much."

"What'd you give Hendricks?"

I started. I thought perhaps I should stop them.

"Oh, God, I feel so sorry for him."

I now recognized their voices. Miss Quist, who'd been assigned to be Honorée's roommate by the computer, and about whom Miss Hogentogler had said to me, "She loves not wisely but too well"; and Miss O'Rourke, a rawboned athlete who, I learned from her life story, had been the women's half-mile champion of S.E. Iowa. She blushed furiously whenever I called on her in class. It was Miss O'Rourke who felt sorry for me. She added, "I feel sorry for him because he tries so hard, you know?"

Miss Quist replied, "Yeah. He wrote all over one of my dumb papers. I mean all over it. He wrote more than I did. Can't you just see him sitting around with nothing better to do than write all over my dumb paper? I wonder about him and girls, you know."

Miss O'Rourke said, "Well, I saw him going into the Huddle, and you know who was with him?"

Miss Quist said, "Yeah, Honorée. That's just because she waitresses there. You want to know something about her? She told me she had a boyfriend in high school and she'd done it with him. And then we talked some and I could tell she was lying like a rug. Then she said she'd gained weight from taking the pill and I asked which doctor she'd gone to and she said her doctor back home. Yeah, well."

Miss O'Rourke must have looked blank, because Miss Quist said, "Would you go to your doctor back home? Well, there. And Honorée comes from a *real* small town. And she won't even use Tampax. But the real way I knew was that she was just lying like a rug."

Miss O'Rourke said, "Well, I feel sorry for her—being so nervous. She talks to herself in class. You can see those big lips of hers waving away if you watch close. And then she makes those little disgusted faces when old Hendricks calls on someone and they're answering. It just drives me nuts. You know another thing? She was a big jock in high school and now she won't talk about it. What a mute!"

I recognized the slang "mute." It did not mean dumb. The nursing students all took an elementary biochemistry course in which the term "mutorotation" occurred. As shortened and adapted to conversational use, it meant "alien," "strange," or, as in this case, "perverse."

I slipped away, keeping the pioneer woman and pedestal between Misses Quist and O'Rourke and me. I'd guessed that Miss Quist didn't like me, although she was strangely flirtatious during our conferences. But I'd thought Miss O'Rourke had a better opinion of me. I had thought of her as a silent heroine— physically powerful and even graceful, but modest and pent up. I imagined she would be a handsome, sympathetic nurse. Perhaps her worse side was only brought out by the venomous Miss Quist, but I was sad to learn there was a worse side.

Honorée came to visit me at my house one Saturday afternoon. She announced the purpose of her visit on the front porch—as though requesting an audience. She was preparing a scene from *Twelfth Night* to audition for an acting class and wished to read it aloud with me.

It was a still, gray day, no color in the sky or in the fields or in the gravel road that looped over the slight rise that separated me from the edge of town. Honorée's face was bright from her walk, and her eyes were shining. She was vividly pretty against the gray day. For that moment I thought it wouldn't be hard to adjust to her simplicity. Simplicity was generally a difficulty for me. I never had any trouble sympathizing with Lear's irritation with Cordelia in Act I. There are of course a great many complications revolving around this point of simplicity, but the only one that I applied then is this: Simplicity that is stubbornly blank is quite different from simplicity that is promising, or at least expectant—cheerfully willing to become part of approaching elaboration, or, as in Honorée's case, advancing itself to be elaborated.

Twelfth Night. Act II, Scene iv. The Duke lectures his page, Cesario (actually Viola disguised as a boy), on love. They listen to a melancholy song sung by the jester. The Duke and Cesario/Viola discuss love. The Duke claims that his love for Olivia (the neighboring beauty he pines for) is heroic as only a man's love can be. Cesario/Viola contradicts him with a sad love story about his (her) sister, that is, herself. Viola is of course in love with the Duke. One of the necessary comic premises is that Viola cannot reveal herself as a girl. The intended delight for the audience in this scene is how close she comes to coming out of her masquerade and how pompously insensible the Duke is. In the end the Duke sends Cesario/Viola traipsing off one more time to Olivia to woo Olivia for him.

I was not flattered when Honorée told me, over tea and oatmeal cookies, that she thought I would be a wonderful Duke. I explained that the Duke is an ass. Honorée said that that couldn't be, since Viola is in love with him.

I said, "Well, let's get on with it, Miss Hogentogler. Perhaps the text will resolve the problem."

She said she knew her part by heart. She gave me her book.

She did know her part, but her acting was all a monotone of yearning. I told her so. I told her there was meant to be some clever playfulness in Viola, not just pathos.

Honorée said with some exasperation, "Well, what do you want me to do, then? Say 'Dukie-wukie, you're a cutie'?"

That made us both laugh.

Honorée got the idea that we could make it funnier if she got dressed up as a boy. I said that she was, insofar as she was wearing pants. She said, "No. You know—in one of your suits."

She nipped off to my bedroom, the only other room in the

house, and returned in my checked three-piece suit. She took my tweed hat from the hook behind the door and tucked her hair up into it. She rolled the pants legs up. It wasn't a grotesque fit. She pulled the back strap on the vest tight so that it was quite trim.

"O.K.," she said. "Let's do this part here. O.K.? You start at 'Once more, Cesario, get thee to yond same sovereign cruelty. . . .' "

I read the speech.

VIOLA   But if she cannot love you, sir?

DUKE   I cannot be so answered.

VIOLA   Sooth, but you must. [Honorée now sounded
          patiently explanatory. Much better.]
          Say that some lady, as perhaps there is,
          Hath for your love as great a pang of heart
          As you have for Olivia: you cannot love her;
          You tell her so; must she not then be
              answered?

DUKE   [I confess I hammed up this speech absurdly.]
          There is no woman's sides
          Can bide the beating of so strong a passion
          As love doth give my heart; no woman's
              heart
          So big to hold so much; they lack retention. . . .

Honorée acted outraged—stood with her fists on her hips, silently mouthing an indignant "What!" Some director must have told her, "Acting is *re*acting."

DUKE   But mine is all as hungry as the sea,
          And can digest as much; make no compare
          Between that love a woman can bear me
          And that I owe Olivia.

VIOLA   [Honorée shifted back to dewy yearning.]
          Ay, but I know—

DUKE   What dost thou know?

VIOLA   Too well what love women to men may owe.
      [Honorée now tried a hearty feigned male
         voice.]
      In faith, they are as true of heart as we.
      My father had a daughter loved a man
      [Back to dewy yearning. In fact, Honorée
         dropped to her knees in front of my
         chair.]
      As it might be, perhaps, were I a woman,
      I should your lordship.

DUKE   And what's her history?

VIOLA   A blank, my lord. She never told her love,
      But let concealment, like a worm i' the bud,
      Feed on her damask cheek: she pined in thought,
      And with a green and yellow melancholy
      She sat like Patience on a monument . . .

I looked up from the text and was surprised to find Honorée's face looming up just below mine. She faltered. She repeated, " '. . . like Patience on a monument . . .' " Her confusion thickened my view of her head, as though I was looking at it through swirls of heat.

VIOLA   . . . Smiling at grief. Was not this love, indeed?

Her confusion now seemed to me to gel into an outer layer of skin, transparent but palpable. I could feel her press it against me as if it were her flesh. I was terrified—if we kissed I would be at fault for this travesty, for this corniness.

VIOLA   [Abruptly back to her male *faux-bourdon*]
      We men may say more, swear more: but indeed
      Our shows are more than will; for still we prove
      Much in our vows, but little in our love.

I said, "Well, that's much better."

Honorée said, "You have some more lines."

"I'm sorry. I lost track."

But Honorée sat back on her heels, satisfied. She said, "That's all right. We did the most important part." She crossed her arms and clasped her elbows. "That was wonderful. I could feel more feeling. Oh, that sounds silly!" She clapped her hands to her forehead and closed her eyes. "Oh, dear!" She lowered her hands to hold her cheeks and looked at me again. "But you know what I mean. You've probably been all through this so many times." Honorée sat back again, this time not on her heels but between them.

"You're very limber," I said.

"Oh, that's part of acting," Honorée said. "I'm auditing body movement. You probably can't tell, but I've lost four pounds. And look at my hands." She held out her hand. "Do you see? I haven't chewed my nails for a week. And—you probably can't tell because I'm being silly now, but I feel older too."

Honorée stayed until suppertime. Since she showed no sign of leaving, I invited her to eat something. She then offered to cook supper. She ended by making a casserole that took an hour and a half to prepare. But the time passed quickly; she listened to records while I read.

Honorée was talkative at supper, much more at ease than during our talks at the Huddle. As usual she asked me a lot of questions, but they seemed less awkward, her curiosity less avid. She also made suggestions: she said I should go for walks along the river—she could show me a path through the woods along the bank. She seemed quite knowledgeable about trees and animals.

By the time we'd finished eating she'd had almost half a bottle of wine. She wasn't drunk, but she was very sweetly looped. I didn't notice until I detected a huskiness in her voice.

It was quite attractive in this new form, much less pinched. It reminded me that she was solidly large in an attractive way— well-sprung ribs, large collarbone, her neck a tower of ivory (as the Song of Songs describes this feature of female beauty, with curiously martial enthusiasm).

I realized that Honorée had been holding herself in in some way—probably trying to look like her roommate, Miss Quist, who was a slinky string bean who expressed herself in small gestures, like cocking one plucked eyebrow, or adjusting her snake hips. Now that Honorée was relaxed, her larger proportions made sense. It was pleasant to think of her voice rising from her deep rib cage through her wide throat, past her big white teeth and full, equal lips. This was the first good aim- less conversation I'd had in a long time. It was very sturdy; nothing could spoil it, not even Honorée saying, "This is so much fun!"

But as we approached the curfew for first-year women students, it became clear that some set code of expectations began to operate. Honorée said, "Oh, don't mind me, I'm just babbling away. I just babble away when I'm having a good time. Most boys don't like that too much. They think talking a lot means you're trying to keep them in their place."

I quoted Malvolio. " 'I would they would know their place as I know mine.' "

Honorée said, "Oh, not that kind of place. Just keeping them from getting too fresh. That's what they *think* it means."

It was ten minutes before curfew when we pulled up to the curb in front of Honorée's dorm. There were swarms of cou- ples on the front steps, spilling over onto the sidewalk and lawn. They were all entwined in one way or another. The effect was that of seeing any natural force deploying itself through individual organisms, each independently but identically pos- sessed by the same ghost of nature—salmon or herring all running upstream to spawn, new-hatched sea turtles scraping across the sand and into the salt water.

My Volkswagen was soon surrounded by couples taking part in this necking frenzy.

I said, "Extraordinary. It wasn't like this in my day."

Honorée giggled. "People kissed good night, didn't they?"

I said, "Well, not *en masse*. Of course, my memory may be dim."

Honorée said severely, "Now don't you talk that way. You pretend to be old, but that's about enough of that."

A couple standing on the walk pressed itself—that is to say, the back of the female half—against the rear side window. At the top of the window I could see the boy's hands pressed between the pane and the girl's back. I felt we were in a diving bell in deep water, seeing deep-sea life.

Honorée said, "You've got to stop talking like that or I'll get cross with you."

A couple walked across our bow, stepping up onto the curb without disconnecting their mouths. Our craft might be swept away by an underwater current of hot kisses.

I said, "In England they call this snogging."

Honorée said, "What do they call snogging? Just kissing?"

"Snogging means necking."

Honorée said, "Snogging," and laughed. She said, "Do people say, 'Let's snog,' or 'May I snog you?' "

The car moved slightly from a readjustment of the couple on our starboard quarter. Honorée noticed it, then pretended not to.

I said, "No. Does this go on every night?"

"Fridays and Saturdays. After January we don't have curfew, so I guess it'll be different after that. But you shouldn't say you're so old. You really shouldn't. I'll bet there're lots of girls who'd like to kiss you."

I said, "Not to the best of my recollection."

"There you go again," Honorée said. "Now I'm really going to get mad at you."

She gave me a playful shove on the shoulder which turned me toward her. She said, "I don't know what I'm going to do with you if you're going to be like that." She put her hands on my shoulders and kissed me.

It was an abrupt movement, but her lips were firmly shut—perhaps puckered—so that my mouth felt it was being jostled by a ripe plum.

My first emotion was surprise, which yielded, surprisingly, to admiration. I should have said something. Whatever Honorée's first feelings, they yielded to embarrassment. She said, "I've got to go. They come out and make you go away at five after." She gathered up her shoulder bag, her book, and her mittens. Her leaving by the passenger door didn't disturb the couple on the fender. They only released me when I revved the motor.

I went to New York for Christmas. I found some of the pleasures I'd been anticipating.

I rode the bus in from La Guardia in a dark massive thrumming of traffic, but once I stepped out of the East Side Terminal the noises of the city were as intelligibly swirled before me as if I were admiring a Jackson Pollock.

The next day it snowed. My parents took me along to a dinner party in Riverdale. We all went Christmas caroling before eating. The Riverdale group had practiced up so that they could do "The First Noel" with descants and harmony. A cozy sight, this group of estimable crisp white-haired Episcopalians carrying blue hymnals, tramping through the slush in black tie and galoshes to carol in each other's driveways, surrounded by snow-capped boxwood and stone walls.

Some of these carolers were good at their jobs. Some of them were intelligent. They were all comfortable in their style, which accommodated a good deal of knowledge. But it was accommodated only; knowledge now seemed to come to them as a guest who might behave well or badly, but who would leave and could be assessed: "Well, I rather liked him."

"Well, I did too, but I don't think we ought to have him back."

"But he'll do very well for the institute."

"Oh, Lord, yes. Just what they're looking for down there."

Many of them—men and women—were trustees. Trustees of hospitals, colleges, museums, schools, nurseries, gardening clubs, cotillions, charities, think tanks. My own mother dealt with unwed mothers. The whole group was like a shadow government for Health, Education, and Welfare. Their trusteeship kept them in touch with life beyond the boxwood.

Shortly after that I went to a party with old schoolmates of mine, many of whom were stretched taut by their first five-year grind as young lawyers. Several of them said they envied my situation. I think one or two of them meant it. As I told one of them about my life in Iowa I could feel it echo back to me: a serene and mysteriously gathered Japanese painting, the reeds of my daily life in the foreground, the almost invisible flat lake of my unmeasured time in the middle distance, and the far-off mountain peak suggesting not challenge or grappling but inevitable extension and completion.

But even the friendliest of these young lawyers wasn't free to be friends with me yet. It wasn't that they only talked shop. It was that they relaxed, after their long hours, by reverting to the schoolboy types they'd been. There was a lot of fast wisecracking—they mocked each other's firms as though they were making old-fashioned Harvard-Yale jokes. They told tales of how severe and bizarre their senior partners were, as though they were comparing Latin masters at St. Mark's and Groton. They treated me better than they had in school, and even inquired politely and literately about my life. But their energy still came from their own wild ride toward success. Talking to them at this party was like talking to them the day before the big game, or the day before college acceptances were mailed. There was a lot of starting-gate humor.

Some of the more reflective admitted that the first several years in a law firm were a period of emotional regression, even though the work occasionally required a high level of competence. Indeed, they knew a great deal more than they had in school, which could in time give them the material for a reflective survey of the world, but at the moment, offering them information was like feeding wild dogs by hand. I heard one lawyer cross-examine a young doctor, a boy who'd been a year behind us at school. The doctor answered fully, only to be torn apart. "Didn't you just say . . ." the lawyer would say, and then make points: The A.M.A. worse than the worst union. A.M.A. worse than worst oil company. Doctors cover up malpractice. Most diseases of unknown origin, cures mostly spontaneous, and yet for this sorry state of affairs doctors have highest per capita income, etc. The lawyer was quite cheerful; he was just practicing. But it was the milk teeth of schoolboy razzing grown into fangs.

These were the brightest of the gang I'd gone through school with. They had come out on top, as I'd hoped they would. Their values, if not their demeanor, were no longer the values of the class bullies and louts, the 1955 cultural commissars. Those unworthies, former seventeen-year-old connivers and hotshots, now developed resorts in Central America or were gynecologists to the suburban rich. This party of lawyers wasn't that old towel-snapping, Coke-squirting, know-nothing clique, the ones who had the power to make me feel that my answers in class were ridiculously pretentious, the ones who left me in such confusion that when I overheard one of my heroes (now at this party) say to one of them, "You know, Hendricks isn't a *total* wimp," I was *pleased*.

This wasn't the locker room or the sixth form common room. It was Latin V taken seriously, but the bell was about to ring for sports. What I now hoped was that between this stage and the Riverdale gentry-and-trustee stage, there would be a stage where we might be joined.

So it was my third social occasion of the holidays that turned out to be the one that comforted me. It was a familiar form of retreat.

Bobby Morse, my old roommate from school, had been, along with me, a not quite total wimp. He'd ended up being saved from wimpiness by two graces. One grace was that he was a slender jock. In fact, he won a prize for being the school's "best non-varsity athlete." A dubious prize, I'd thought, but then, no one is harder on a near-wimp than a fellow near-wimp. Bobby was a passable recreational tennis player and skier, but he was a very good figure skater. Imagine being a figure skater at a New England boarding school in the 1950s. But one day early in the winter of our fifth form year, the hockey coach invited Bobby to join the hockey players in a race the length of the rink. The coach was cannier than I was— I foresaw only humiliation for Bobby. Bobby beat them all three times in a row—in a straight end-to-end race; around a tight circle; and in a figure eight that looped around both goal cages. The coach thanked Bobby calmly, and posted Bobby's times in the locker room. By midseason several of the hockey players were up to his times, but Bobby wasn't interested.

Bobby's other saving grace was his sister, Antoinette.

During his fourth form year she was a senior at a nearby girls' school. Bobby and Antoinette entered amateur figure-skating contests in the pairs competition. Sometimes they practiced on the pond at her school, but when the pond ice wasn't good, then the hockey coach let them use the rink at our school. The older boys who contrived to hang around were goggle-eyed. In those days one didn't see a girl's legs above the calf except in summer, and the sight of Antoinette speeding backward, her apparent wind flipping her skating tutu up from her rear-jutting rump tight-clothed in the underpart of her scarlet costume, was enough to dazzle the boys hanging over the rails. The hockey coach would clear them out periodically, but they'd drift back. I think the coach had a sly crush on her too, though he genuinely fancied figure skating. Antoinette thought the boys absurd, which was a comfort to me, but her caustic attitude to these raw males also made her very much an older sister to me.

Being with Antoinette and Bobby then, and off and on during the year between, and now in New York, was all one piece. Even though we had separate stories to tell, the controlling tone of our sheltered intimacy was fixed. My attitudes toward my parents, toward boarding school, college, and graduate school, toward almost any figure in my life, had changed. When we three were together, however, I felt that our association contained both those moments of adolescence when one is suddenly the person one will be at thirty, and also those moments of the present and future when one is most like the person one has always been.

Bobby and Antoinette now shared an apartment almost as big as my parents'. I'd been there once before, a year earlier. It was due west of my parents' place, across the park. If we'd still been in school, Bobby and I would have signaled each other by flashing mirrors.

Although Bobby and I had been outsiders together, he had a happier nature than mine. It was he who offered to make friends with me. I put him off at first because once we became friends our fate would be doubly sealed; neither of us would be promoted. But he had no interest in promotion, neither his nor mine. After we became friends, I found out he had trumps he hadn't played. Even in fourth form—that is, in 1953—he'd been to the Folies Bergère. He could have regaled the regular gang with even the simplest anatomical information. And I suspect he had more experiences in France (where his father lived) than he told even me. He regarded—rightly, it turned

out—the then American teen-age attitudes toward women as
competitive, unfeeling, spiteful, and irredeemably uninformed.
He was—wrongly, it turned out—completely baffled by American girls.

He was almost as thin as I was, though, of course, physically more skillful. But he lost some of the prestige his minor
sports might have won for him by his lack of vehemence. When
he played tennis, it didn't seem like an athletic event. And
when he practiced figure skating by himself during the winter,
even I thought it looked more absurd than graceful, especially
because he would walk down to the ice rink in sealskin boots
with little tassels which seemed to me alarmingly froufrou.

He was a good friend to me, and a wonderfully pleasant
roommate—spontaneously neat, but not fussy; generous with
chocolate, books, and information. He was entirely candid with
me about his family. I'd at first imagined his mother as an
elegant Frenchwoman—a countess at least. He casually dis-
abused me. He liked his father but saw quite plainly that his
father had run out of energy. Bobby's great-grandfather had
made a lot of money in farm machinery in Iowa. His grand-
father had moved to Chicago and enlarged the business—he'd
bought a patent on an early version of the ready-made gas-fired
corn-drying silo. Bobby and Antoinette's father had gone to
France in the thirties, got married, had Antoinette and Bobby.
The war started. Bobby's mother moved to London, the father
ended up interned in Paris. The mother took up with another
American. Antoinette and Bobby lived in Devonshire. The
mother stayed in London. The father got the children back
after the war. He was now an art dealer who lived in Paris and
New York, but, as Bobby readily admitted, his father didn't
really understand painting. He provided some capital, and he
had a smart French partner. He liked living in Paris, spoke
French fluently with a happily American accent, made friends
there. He put his children in American boarding schools when
they were young, but picked them up for every vacation. He

spoke to them more openly than any other parent I knew. The effect on them was that they thought every other parent they met was more mysterious and powerful than their father.

My mother adored Bobby. One time when he was fourteen he spent the night with us. His father dropped him off and stayed for a drink. Later that evening my mother said to Bobby, "What a nice man your father is!" Bobby was thrilled. It was the first time an American grownup from the group with whom he was being educated took a visible interest in his father.

His father struck me as remarkably placid. He was older than my parents but appeared younger. He wore well-shined loafers and a very soft sports jacket. I thought it was his calm my mother liked. A couple of years later I figured out she had meant to please Bobby.

On the other side of this equation, Antoinette was equally affectionate toward me. When Bobby and I had gone to different colleges, it was she who made the administrative effort to keep Bobby and me friends. She would send me postcards telling me when Bobby and she would be in New York on their way to Paris—the hotel, the room number. After she graduated from college and moved to New York, she would invite us to supper at her apartment. This was when she was just starting out, before her accident.

I had been smitten by her, but no more so than by any glamorous woman. She did a little modeling, but was already in the business end when she went through the windshield in a car crash. Her face was repaired in a series of operations and wirings.

The first time I saw her after she was fixed up and healed, I thought she was still pretty. She had a slight depression in her right temple, beyond the end of her eyebrow. Her right masseter was now marginally smaller than the left. Whether because of the reduced masseter or some reduction in supporting bone, there was also a hollow in her jaw and chin which gave the impression that her face curved very slightly to the right. She openly referred to her face as being crescent-shaped. This was an exaggeration, but her joking about it in this way misled me. I was then a senior in college, but it seemed only a short while before that Antoinette had been my comforter in the matter of cousin Josie. Antoinette had said, "She's too dumb for you, Oliver. I'm pretty mean, but if you'd written poems to me I would have been nicer than that log-brain." So (seven years later) I wrote out a bit of doggerel on the subject of Antoinette's altered beauty, referring to her new-moon face (which was her idea, after all), and ending up with the admittedly unoriginal thought that the allure of flawed beauty was better than austere perfection.

I presented this in person. She unfolded it and read it without expression. She refolded the sheet, put it back in the envelope, and handed it to me. I said, with puzzled brightness, "No, it's for you."

She said, "I'm afraid not."

She may have meant to be gentler, but I fled.

When I reread it in the light of her displeasure, I couldn't figure out how I could have been so inept.

Bobby and Antoinette and I had a long-standing engagement the next day. Antoinette and I were embarrassed to see each other.

She said, "I'm sorry. I shouldn't have. I've been depressed in some dumb way, and I seem to have misplaced my sense of humor."

And I—like the fairy-tale princess under a spell who when she opens her mouth to speak emits a toad—said, "Oh. But it wasn't meant to be funny."

But in some way Antoinette felt herself to blame, and so finally this short embarrassment of which she and I each held an end turned into an odd sort of intimacy. The outlaw bond (outlaw because Bobby had no vanity—neither my pretension to art nor Antoinette's prickly reflex about her looks) was only part of it. We found we had several subjects in common. Antoinette was a great one not only for keeping up with contemporary goings on but also for classical self-improvement. Having gone to Wellesley (she spent her junior year in France) and worked hard, she was already literate. She practiced no art and pursued no single scholarly discipline, but she would take up small subjects with cranky zest that might last several months. The history of the papacy, Turkish rugs, the Gulf Stream, Yeats, Vikings, Elizabethan lyrics, New York real estate. All these in addition to a steady interest in fashion (her job), fine arts (her college major), and French literature (her college minor).

I was her literary consultant. We went to whatever was playing in New York—there was always something—but the field on which we met with equality was Molière, a playwright to whom she was temperamentally sympathetic. It was also to Antoinette that I owed my instruction in La Rochefoucauld and Chamfort.

But our main subject was always Bobby. I was her consultant in that case too. She continued to make sure that Bobby and I got together at least twice a year. I once suspected that this was one of her hobbies—a kind of gardening of two sympathetic crops. But as well as her cool assessment and administration, there was also a feverish tenderness. Sometimes when Antoinette and I first saw each other, she would seize my hands and speak in a rapid monotone, saying how glad she was I'd come, how worried she'd been about Bobby, about her father. As she spoke, her fingers would move over my knuckles and wrist bones, as though my joints were the knobs of an instrument transmitting her real message.

When I first went to their apartment this Christmas break, she went through this nervous telegraphy at the door. Then, soothed by her transmission, she took me into the living room and relaxed into an armchair by the window. She gave a little laugh and started talking about Bobby as though we'd all seen each other the day before and an amusing addition to our conversation had just occurred to her.

She said, "I've just figured out how it works with Bobby and his girl friends."

The pattern she mapped out was this: Every so often Bobby would meet a young woman who'd recently arrived in Manhattan and was overwhelmed by small difficulties. For a month or two he would spend his spare time solving her problems—perhaps helping her find an apartment, explaining the subway, recommending a doctor. After that he might let himself into her place with his spare key to leave a house plant, to install an extra lock, or thumbtack a useful magazine article to her bulletin board.

Bobby and his *ingénue* (Antoinette's term) would go out twice a week. Once in a while he would spend the night. Antoinette was sure that they weren't in love because she could see nothing but amiable good moods in either of them, and only slight wistfulness toward the end. The end began when Bobby introduced the *ingénue* to men and women who he thought would be likely friends for her. Since almost all the past heroines of these interludes remained friendly with Bobby, the latest *ingénue* usually met one of her predecessors. This introduction marked the very end.

They were not desperate women. They all had jobs or plausible competences or enough money to go back home. What bothered Antoinette wasn't that this was a vice—at least not in the sense that it did any harm to the woman. But she didn't like the fact that Bobby was so expert at the little problems that inevitably repeated themselves each time. She said that it gave the whole operation the aura of a hobby. I thought it an indication of how close we were that "having a hobby" struck us both as a phrase for an unworthiness in someone we cared about.

Antoinette said, "I wish it wasn't so boring for him to make money. Or maybe I wish he'd take one of these women seriously. He's just taken up with the best one ever, but he's not even trying as hard as usual. If he's not going to fall in love, I wish he had some other devotion. I sometimes wish he'd worked things out the way you have—what you do all day and what you like are one thing."

I said that there was still a lot missing from my life.

She said, "But you're getting somewhere. You're adding to what you know, not doing the same thing over and over. Bobby repeats everything. His books, his making money, his girl friends."

I asked how Bobby's life was different from her own. She chose not to hear this as a rude question.

She said, "I may not be doing any better, but I keep planning to do better. Bobby seems half-heartedly content."

I agreed that it was certainly true that Bobby lacked the divine discontent.

But when we went out to dinner, Bobby showed up with his friend. It turned out I knew her—not an *ingénue* at all in my view. She'd been one of the stars of graduate school in comparative literature when I'd been working on my Ph.D. in English. Elizabeth Mary Chetty. She'd come from India in the first place, but after much traveling had passed through Europe and ended up at Harvard. She surprised me now by recognizing me. I thought she'd been too hard at work to notice anyone, though she herself was well known as the darling of the most difficult seminars.

When I'd known Elizabeth Mary—or, more accurately, observed her—I had even come to dislike her in a petty way, the way one falls into disliking anyone who's the center of attention. Now, as she greeted me with a tone of pleasant surprise, of course my feelings immediately fell at her feet.

Elizabeth Mary still had traces of Indian accent—not the exuberant quasi-Welsh singsong, but a fluid hurdling of each emphasized word. Hearing one of her spoken paragraphs was like listening to an expertly run quarter mile of intermediate hurdles. Her whole voice neatly tucked up its lower register, skimmed over, then was in full stride again, gathering its silky rush and hum for the next flit of emphasis.

I was so taken with the laps her voice was making that I lost track of the subject. I remember her saying that Americans had humor but no wit and my not wanting to argue. Then I was admiring her narrow dark gold nose, when there was a silence and I realized she'd been asking me something about Iowa. While I was trying to think of something to mumble, it came echoing back to me that she'd just said she was going to teach there for a term. I guessed that she must be asking about either the faculty or the students. I said, "Well, there's a spread. It's hard for me to say; you may find something quite different."

"Oh, Oliver," Elizabeth Mary said. "Come right out and tell me the worst. I am prepared for any kind of illiteracy."

I gathered it was students she was after. I said, "There are a few who are eager." And I told her several Honorée Hogentogler stories.

Walking back to the Morses' apartment, Antoinette slipped her arm through mine and slowed us down so that we lagged behind Bobby and Elizabeth Mary.

Antoinette said, "I'm afraid Bobby is introducing you to her. I'd hoped he was completely serious about her. She'd be so good for him."

I said that I thought Bobby just wanted me to be polite to her for her one-term visit. I added, "When I'm out there I'm devoted to Miss Hogentogler. And when I'm here, you're my ideal."

Antoinette wasn't much of a flirt. She said, "Oliver, that's like loving your nanny."

It was in this foursome that I had a pretty good time until it was time to fly back to Iowa. Each of us knew enough about a variety of arts and entertainments and about the taste of the others to be able to make something of a week of afternoons and evenings.

But as soon as I drove out of the parking lot of the Cedar Rapids airport, I was despondent. It wasn't the three weeks of the fall term trailing into January. It was the first tremor in my major hopes. I had felt until then that all I had to do was keep up with my program of cultural and spiritual progress and I would inevitably reach way stations where there would be other people into whose clarified sensibilities I would be able to see. I had felt that all the efforts I had made toward the fragments of the past (including those whole works I loved most) would be rewarded in the future by whole sensibilities. As every idea anyone had ever formulated about a work of art fell short, was a weak caged specimen of the power of the art at large, so art itself fell short of the power of sensibility in its highest state.

And if one wished to dismiss this idea, one would have only an idea about an idea, which would be devoid of even the caged power of an idea. So this core of belief in progress toward communion had always been at a safe remove from thought.

But of course the danger of belief removed from thought is that it may recklessly add to itself or be added to (who could tell?). At that moment there was certainly some unbalancing or corroding element in my belief.

I had just told stories about Honorée Hogentogler—her laughable tumbling eagerness. Driving through the countryside, I thought that I might be laughable too; Honorée and I might be sisters under the skin.

There was a dull twilight, the rising moon behind a scrim of clouds, the setting sun curtained off by thicker clouds, the light spread about unevenly by the snow incompletely covering the ground. The farmhouses, buildings, and machinery visible from the highway looked makeshift, and only half in use, as though a city had toppled and these were the farthest-flung pieces reassembled. Turkish goat pens made of the ruined stubs of Ionic columns. This regressive and mean vision passed before I pulled into my driveway. In my mailbox was a card from Honorée. A New Year's card. It was a picture of her coming into a room wearing a white gown and a crown of lighted candles. She wrote: "My father used this for his bank's calendar. I'm January and my sister is February. See you soon. Love, Honorée."

She looked embarrassed and very pretty. A birthday cake too pretty to be cut.

I went into my office the next day and at lunchtime went to the Huddle. Honorée was there. She came around the counter and kissed me on the cheek. She seemed stronger and more expansive—I'd been thinking of the picture on the New Year's card, in which she seemed delicate.

She said, "I wouldn't have done that except it's my last day here. I get to quit my job. My dad said I'd showed I could do it and now I'll have time to work on a movie. I'll tell you about that in a second. Did you get the card?"

I nodded and said it was very pretty.

She said, "That was taken last year. My mom's so corny about that stuff. She came from Minnesota."

I looked puzzled.

Honorée said, "They do more of those Swedish things there. Anyway, things have been hectic. You know my roommate, Miss Quist? Well, she told me before vacation that she was going to room with somebody else next term and so the dorm supervisor's letting me live in a single room in approved housing. That's just one thing. And then I got into the acting class and there's this TA who's making a movie. It's just a little farce but he got a grant to do it and I get to be in it. It's silent, but anyway the main thing is the theater crowd here are so nice. I'd heard—Karen Quist told me—that they were snobby, but they've been terrific. This TA said I could be in his improv group. It's the same crowd he's making the movie with. Last year they did the experimental one-act that won the student contest. It's their own technique; it's very practical—sort of avant-garde Marx Brothers. A lot of physical clowning. Last term the TA substitute taught body movement one time and that's where he saw me. He said it was good the way I did falls. The secret of good farce is really precision that surprises, and he said it was surprising that I could move so well."

I said, "I hope this doesn't take too much time away from your work."

"Oh, no. I had good grades at midterm. If I do as well on midyears, I'll have a three point six."

I found all this news, or rather Honorée's exhilaration about it, hard to fit in. After she'd come out to visit me and I'd driven her back to her dorm, I'd been afraid I would have to have a talk with her. She'd seemed innocent and helpless in her aspiration to what she thought of as college life—the whole corny turmoil that I'd skipped but which I was afraid she hoped to find in me. And I'd been troubled by our kiss. I'd had a clear sense of Honorée by sight and sound, and then these two known languages had been complicated by the third, as though I'd turned the Rosetta stone and found a hieroglyph which I wasn't sure I wished to translate.

And I'd had other ambiguous thoughts about her when I hadn't been busy assessing my New York life. One of these unbidden visions of her was particularly persistent for all its absurdity. The plot was that Honorée had been left on my doorstep as a child and then suddenly grown into a lovely pliant child who kept me company. This Silas Marner fantasy was as embarrassing to me as any of the other moments of embarrassment that popped into my head from my real life, dumb things that I'd said years before—for example, some attempted elegance that had failed and which could still make me suck in my breath with shame.

And yet this guardian mode was the one that kept floating to the top. I'd entertained the idea of heartlessly abusing her trust, of accepting what pleased me from her affections while remaining free to shake her off. I had no absolute scruple—certainly not a notion of an eternal father sending a thunderbolt or shower of frogs to punish my lust. I could easily imagine that there was such a plausible mode as the carefree rake, a jolly scoundrel who could take pleasure because he gave pleasure, no cobwebs of feeble piety. But I knew that was not my sensibility. That essentially comic role would take either more energy or less energy than I spent in my life, but certainly a different kind of energy.

Honorée said, "When I was two or three, my mother claims, I had a Swedish accent. We went to church for a Christmas pageant and I looked at all the girls dressed up like angels carrying candles and I said, 'Look, Mama! Dere's a yady with a yight. And dere's anudder yady with a yight.'" Honorée laughed at her singsong. She said, "I dreamed about that. Except you were there and you could really talk Swedish and that made my mother really happy. Except later on in that dream, or maybe it was another dream, I had to go to a party and everyone but me was speaking in blank verse. Just like *Twelfth Night*. They'd even say a rhymed couplet before they'd exit. It was really awful. But I think I know what that's about—it was my anxiety about the theater crowd. And *that's* not a problem anymore. I don't know why I didn't have any confidence this fall. I guess I thought there was just one way to be good at things—there was a set of rules, and either you knew or you didn't. You know, the way Miss Quist just seemed to know what was O.K. and how to do things. But then I saw you just going ahead and being the way you were and talking about the way you thought and not caring about whether that made you popular. And then talking to you by myself, I saw you were completely sincere about the way you were in class. Well, that was one thing I learned—that you don't need to be heartbroken about anything. Someone will appreciate you. You were so nice about that—well, not really nice, because that would mean you weren't sincere about what you think of me.

"And now everything's just sailing along. Just think. If all this can happen before the first year's even over, what'll the next three years be like?"

I had a sudden sense of Honorée's sensation of her life then—prettily piled-up clouds sailing by on a short spring day.

I went back to my office, where I found my Okie officemate moving his things out. He was embarrassed. "Did you get my note?" he said. "I'm just going down the hall. I'm moving in with the guy that uses a lot of the same books. I left a note in the mailbox; I wasn't sure you'd be back so early. Your mail's all there still. This is going to work out better for our schedules —I was always getting in your hair."

I said something amiable.

He lifted his carton of books and notes with his typewriter perched on top. I asked if I could help carry the typewriter.

"No; thanks anyway." He said, "Well, I sure won't miss the view." We both laughed. The view was of the parking lot. Actually, I rather liked looking down on the parking lot—it was the one place one could see the coming and going of the Easter parade. But I wanted to be polite.

I lost myself in typing, a mindless anthill task. Insect tedium, carrying one grain of sand after another under a sky that was too vast.

I read my office mail when I got home. My feelings were less hurt—my ex-officemate had written a nice note. There was also a Christmas card from Honorée, which she'd mailed before vacation. Santa and his reindeer landing on the roof of a house. She'd written: "At least it's not an airplane."

I called her to ask her to come out for supper on Saturday. She said, "Oh," several times and then said she couldn't. We both hung up with surprise.

When I picked up the phone a little later to ask her to come Friday instead, two women were talking on the party line.

I heard one speak with what I thought was unnatural

slowness. "Did you get to that sale I told you about before? I got to it right at the end . . . and I bought . . ." She listed a dozen things and their prices. The agonizing stretch of speech and pause depressed me. But I didn't hang up. The other woman spoke, even more slowly than the first. "I got there all right." She described in detail who had taken her in which car by what roads. She said, "You know what Jim said . . . when I told him . . . about buying a new bra? He said, 'You know what they call them now? They call them over . . . the . . . shoulder . . . boulder . . . holders.' "

There was a long pause and then both women laughed. There was another pause of a slow breath and they laughed again. The second woman repeated the phrase and, after another pause, laughed.

The first woman said, "There's Jim coming back now. I guess I got to go."

They fixed a time when they would speak again and finally hung up.

Honorée said she couldn't come for supper on Friday but she would come out Friday afternoon.

I stepped outside and strolled around the yard.

I remembered my landlord showing me the house, slowly explaining how to take down the screens and put up the storm windows. We went to the basement. Behind the furnace there was a sawhorse, and across it there was balanced a long saw with a handle at either end. My landlord said, "So that's where that got to. Last time we used that was cutting a fence post on V-J day."

Now I thought of that saw balancing for twenty slow years.

I looked at the line of road, at the flat ridge along which a tractor moved as slowly as a cloud. The sky was still.

I had an attack of agoraphobia—not just a fear of open space, but of open time, a fear of the slowness of the woman's comfortable speech, of time expanding until all incident, all definition, and all rhythm were diminished. My thought was of

less importance than my breathing, which, mysteriously, refused the panic in my mind. Breath followed breath, infinitely
small fractions of an invisible cloud troubling nothing.

I recovered by Honorée's visit on Friday afternoon. I'd
received a note from Elizabeth Mary Chetty announcing when
she was arriving to spend the spring term. The thought of her
tropically dense intelligence gave me pleasure. This anticipated
pleasure settled me. Honorée came out in a pickup truck she'd
borrowed. Because she hadn't walked out, she said we had to go
for a long walk. With her as my guide, the landscape didn't seem
dangerously transient but a simple well-behaved background to
her childish prettiness. Honorée's walking tour took us across
the nearest field and into the woods to a stream. On the way
across the field, she pointed out rabbit tracks in the snow.

She said, "Look. Here he's just walking along. And then
here he starts to run. See how the two front paws are together
and he's really jumping with his back legs. That's those long
tracks right there. And over there you can see how he zig-
zagged. And then they end here. If you look right there and
there you can see why."

"Why?"

Honorée pointed to two faint brushings in the snow about
a pace apart. "Those are from the wingtips of an owl. Maybe a
hawk, but more likely an owl. That little hole in the snow in
between the wings is where he got caught. An owl doesn't just
snatch, you know—they open up their claws so they just stick
straight in. Their wings open up right at the end of their dive to
keep them from crashing. They don't want to land at all—it's
hard for them to take off from the ground, they're so big."

I found this narrative of signs sad, but Honorée was filled
with good humor and energy. She bounced around the woods
in her gum boots as though she were dancing. She bent a sapling down to the ground and rode it like one end of a seesaw. It
didn't work very well. She dismounted and let the sapling go.

She said, "When I was little, my father would pull over a

green tree like this and I'd go flying right up into the air. My father was the one who got me interested in modern dance."

I said, "I thought you were a gymnast in high school."

Honorée said, "Oh—yes; that was the nearest thing to it in that high school. But my father drove us down to the next town for modern dance every Saturday. His only fault was that he thought we were all wonderful. That's why I couldn't trust him after a while, because he'd always say I was wonderful no matter what. But it was good to be encouraged, I guess. You remind me of my father some. Except of course you don't exactly overpraise me—but that's good. The way you decide something's good or bad is so definite, so when you finally do decide something's good it isn't just because you like some person. And of course it works the other way around too—you could tell me something I've done isn't any good and I wouldn't be worried that you didn't like me."

She gave a tug at the sapling. "I think it's not really springy enough because it's winter."

I thought her appreciation of me was false—rather like a nineteenth-century picture-book version of the Middle Ages. But it didn't matter for the moment; we were alternating in a pleasant pretty way, as though we were singing two different songs in a round—"Frère Jacques" and "Row, Row, Row Your Boat."

We had tea and watched the sun set. She seemed to have a good idea of how pleased I was by her visit. It made her more articulate; I'd known she had a sense of humor but I hadn't realized she had a precise, and at times even skeptical, intelligence. She also had a sweetly bossy side—advising me to eat more, to lower the heat in my house so I wouldn't catch cold from going out overheated.

She suddenly stood up. "Oh, my gosh. I've got to be at the theater. We all have to see this Marx Brothers movie together. Oh, they'll hate it if I'm late."

I said I'd give her a ride.

She laughed. "I drove myself out." She said, "Don't you notice what's sitting in your own yard?" She pointed out the window to the pickup truck. For some reason my absent-mindedness embarrassed me. Honorée had been about to laugh again, but stopped when she noticed my expression. Her attention embarrassed me more, an embarrassment now absurdly out of proportion to a trivial cause.

I thought Honorée was peering at me, and even seeing for the first time that I had a nervous flaw.

But she said, "Oh. Don't worry. You don't have to give me a ride to get your kiss."

I was surprised by this now perfect misunderstanding. And now Honorée, having surprised herself, blushed up to her eyes. We looked at each other. She was stopped dead, no momentum of teasing to help her. More slowly than I would have ever imagined, she moved upstream against the current of my look. She was still nervous, but solemnly certain of giving pleasure. As she slid her feet forward, she took a shallow breath through her nose that made her head bob. We kissed, and then Honorée relaxed completely, as though her curiosity, her duty, her worry, her expectation, were all lifted up. She leaned on me happily for an instant, as though she was a castaway washed ashore on me by a long wave. It was really her pleasure and trust that touched me. For a short while I thought that was all there was to it, that all I had to be was the shore soothed by the wave.

I slowly worked my way through my piles of blue books and final term papers. I also had to sit on a committee which reviewed a number of the examinations graded by teaching assistants.

At the end of this miserable week I drove to the Cedar Rapids airport to pick up Elizabeth Mary Chetty. The department chairman seemed impressed that I knew her. I felt as though I'd won a prize when she moved in to share my office.

She seemed glad to see me, and soon had me convinced that we were old chums. She was as argumentative as ever, but now that we were suddenly friends I found I even liked her retrospectively. I could now cluck amiably and familiarly at her brilliant wrong-headedness, rather than feel shriveled at the thought of her heresies being rewarded.

Our basic disagreement was this: She regarded criticism as the highest form of creative amalgamation. She wished to swoop down on the wings of theory from her aerie on a timeless mountain and carry off her prey, whose most edible innards she called "structures." She in her turn regarded me as a worm, writhing around forever in "the period," munching my way through even the third- and fourth-rank writers, provided they smelled and tasted like "the period."

We insulted each other merrily. She would say, "Oh, Oliver —you are nothing but an encomiast. You are nothing but an aestheticizer. You wish to preserve the innocence of everything and everybody. If only you could insinuate yourself into the brain of some typical Elizabethan groundling actually seeing a Shakespeare play then and there, you would think you'd found the truth. That is how puny it is to be 'true to the age.' "

And I would say that she loved dangerous ideas just because they were dangerous and that her theories were nothing but jujitsu holds and that she was only happy when an author was at her feet.

I confess that she was more consistent with her simple worm metaphor than I was with my eagle and jujitsu.

She said, "There. Now we both have said the very worst. I feel good enough to go back to work. And please don't tempt me into chatting when we are in our office together; there it must be work, work, work."

Within two days of her arrival she was swamped with applicants for her upper-level seminar. She ruthlessly chucked out all but the brightest. I was impressed with her quick scan of who they were. The next day she invited me along to lunch with two senior members of the department. She was brilliantly chatty. She alluded to their works shamelessly. She took the major theory in one senior colleague's book and wiggled it like a loose tooth. The colleague whose tooth it was was seized with the sensation which he finally decided was pleasurable.

The next day both senior members showed up for the first lecture of her survey course, giving it an air of grand occasion as they tried to make themselves unobtrusive, settling into the cushioned seats of the lecture hall, their scarves dangling around their necks like albs. The students beside them stuffed their own snow-sogged parkas and field jackets aside, away from the ranking overcoats. The senior presences made soothing gestures with their fingers, meaning don't mind me, don't bother, just dropping in.

Several students handed out mimeographed sheets—the reading list, the next twenty lecture topics with keyed reading assignments, and a detailed outline of the day's lecture.

All these formal details, I saw with some envy, roused the students to a state of nervous attention. Elizabeth Mary didn't let it lapse. I was surprised at her tone. She wasn't at all playful now—in fact, she seemed not only totally serious but furious. So furious and concentrated did she seem that it took me a while to realize that she wasn't going very fast. Quite right for a middle-level survey. This wasn't a dissection of the nervous system of the work she was discussing—rather a carving of the several large muscles and bones. And she certainly had no trouble finding the joints.

Several days later I suggested to her that she'd had no trouble finding the joints in the local corpus of authority either. She turned her elegant attention on me.

"Shall I give you a piece of advice, Oliver? I am amusing myself here, and I shall soon be gone to fresh fields and pastures new. But I would like to help you. It is not enough for you to just work, work, work. It is not even enough for you to have an idea that bursts like a bombshell. What one in your case must do is this—one presents one's ideas quite fiercely, aiming quite directly at the established positions of someone quite important. But then it is absolutely crucial that one has a good chat afterward with this important fellow. One does not back down—not at all. But one makes it clear that one sees his points and that one is given pause. Then, after several days during which one is visibly knitting one's brows, one has another chat and one admits that certain restatements and even revisions are being considered most seriously. Either of two things may happen. One"—she held up one slender toasted finger—"one is seen as the harbinger of new ideas, but in the guise of loyal opposition, not as some rude radical. Or two"—she held up another finger—"one is seen as a possible convert well worth the converting. One is not listened to if one is only muttering one's ideas to oneself and keeping out of sight. Even your own Bible tells you it is better to be the one lost sheep rather than the ninety-nine silly sheep who are staying quietly in the fold."

I said, "So that's the secret."

Elizabeth held up her whole hand and said, "Are you being arch with me, Oliver? You can be very sweet or you can be a little bit sour. I am in perfectly good faith with you. This advice would not be of use unless one has done one's work. It would be of no use at all if one were not serious." She rose suddenly, took two steps, and stood over me. She patted the back of my hand sharply and then let her fingertips rest on it. "You have an interesting sensibility, Oliver, and I think it is going to blossom in a most intricate way." I was deeply, deeply charmed.

Honorée came by the next day to ask me to approve her application to "test out" of her second half of the required composition course. I said I would miss her in class.

She said, "Well, don't be sad. I'll still drop by to say hi, for heaven sakes."

We discussed her courses. It turned out she was taking Elizabeth Mary's survey course. I asked Honorée how she liked it.

She said, "Miss Chetty's just wonderful. That's who I'd really like to be like. I'd carry a torch for her."

I said, "Carry a torch?"

She said, "You know—lead a parade."

I explained to her what carrying a torch means.

"Oh, dear," Honorée said. "I thought it was like a torch in a ceremony, like the Olympic Games. Oh, dear." She put her hand over her mouth and giggled through it. "I'm glad it was you I said it to. I might have said it in public."

I said, "So. Now that you're an actress you care more for your public. Your movie part has gone to your head."

Honorée blushed. "Oh, *that*. But you know what I mean. I mean I don't care your knowing some silly details about me because you know everything about the way I am really."

I was suddenly touched by her. I could feel her efforts to ascend, and there was a surge of sympathetic aspiration in me, a bright echo of her buoyancy. Her full face appeared inspired, her large eye sockets like great rose windows in a new church. She gave her nervous laugh, looked away, composed her face, and looked back at me, chewing her lower lip. My saying nothing made her more nervous than my schooling her.

She said, "Well, I'll see you in class."

I said, "Well, if you're going to test out there's not much point."

She said, "Well, if I don't I don't want to fall behind."

Our next class, it was Miss Quist's turn to do "My Favorite Magazine."

"My Favorite Magazine," Miss Quist said. "My favorite

magazine is *College Girl*. I've tried *Cosmopolitan, Seventeen,* and *Glamour* and *Mademoiselle*, and let's face it—*College Girl* gets right to work for us girls from the Midwest. Girls in other parts of the country don't have the problems we do. Southern belles have something going for them—all those books and movies. And everyone thinks California girls are tan all over. [*Laughter from the class*] So let's say you're a nice girl from a small town in the Midwest and you want to get in on the fun. Well, there's this one column in *College Girl* that gives you game plans. Just about everyone in my dorm has picked up a move or two from this column.

"Here's a summary of one article I know has been helpful for a certain kind of girl.

"Let's say you're not getting a rush from the college boys. Let's say your first year in college is as dull as your last year in high school. What does college have that high school doesn't? A lot more men, that's what! So what if you can't get in with the kids who go out for pizza and beer after the football game. There are lots of men at a college who have other interests— from astronomy to zoology. A lot of these guys are perfectly nice and there's nothing wrong with them just because they're a little bit older. So what if they've spent the last five years reading Latin and Greek. Someone's going to wake them up sometime and it might as well be you.

"So how do you start? You ask him for help. You say, 'I'm sorry, but you seem to have the only copy of Dante's *Inferno* in Italian. Then you say, 'No, I don't speak Italian. I just wanted to see what it looked like.' Then you say, 'Oh, you do! Would you read some to me?' And then you close your eyes.

"Tell him it was deeply moving, but be sure you go away soon. Just a spoonful of this stuff at a time. It's awful rich and you don't want to upset him.

"If you drop by his office or library cubbyhole to ask him to recommend some reading, remember, don't ever stay too long: always have somewheres else to go. Cinderella didn't get the prince to come looking for her by being the last to leave the party.

"And then when you get him to explain such and such a part of his recommended reading, you might argue just a teensy bit, but in the end you say, 'Oh! Oh, I *see!*'

"Now, these grad students and instructors are a little different from your normal Joe College in some little ways. Here's a little hint that should suggest the kind of delicate treatment you should use. Let's say you've got to the point where you've got to leave a note on his door, or under his door, or with the department secretary. Don't—*do not!*—put it in a pink envelope with big girlish handwriting. Typed address on a plain envelope, puh-leez. This subspecies of male doesn't go for holding hands in public either. He may not even want to appear in public with you. He's not ashamed of you—he's just shy. Intellectually he may be a graybeard, but emotionally he may be younger than you are.

"Take some walks. Get him outdoors and tell him how much better he looks with color in his cheeks. He'll begin to think you're what's good for his health."

It was not until this point that I realized what Miss Quist was up to. If I hadn't overheard her talking to Miss O'Rourke, I might not have understood. I had moved to the back row for Miss Quist's speech. Honorée was sitting in the front row but I could see that her neck and arms were tense.

Miss Quist moved on in her march to the sea. She said, "This particular article of this particular column for this kind of girl even gave some more tips. It said that you couldn't just stick to academic topics, but you could always count on holding a man's interest by getting him to tell stories about how he got started in his interests and how he had a hard time because the other kids thought he was a bookworm.

"Well, you can certainly see how helpful this sort of advice could be in building up confidence for a particular sort of reader. I'm not going to tell you what article it was in this column that gave me some of my ideas, but it was helpful to me too along those different lines that might interest me. So that's why *College Girl* is my favorite magazine. Thank you."

I would like to be able to say that I crushed Miss Quist. That I said, "It is clear that you were speaking of Miss Hogentogler and me, but you fell short, as envy and malice will always fall short. As envy and malice will always be too small to know the truth." And so forth.

I have even imagined that I should have said, "Miss Hogentogler, will you be my wife?" and that that perfect gesture would have filled us both with such sympathy that each of us would have understood the other's life in such a way that we could have lived it.

I realize that by having this extravagant fantasy of impossible rightness, I am only trying to avoid facing the smaller possibilities that existed then to have done something good. As it was, I let the moment pass in a muddle. I think I was even frightened by the glitter of Miss Quist's wicked nerve.

I remember thinking that I had seen a flash of envy that lighted up something I hadn't ever quite understood—that is, Iago. I made a note of this small perception.

Honorée left a note in my mailbox saying she'd successfully "tested out."

For a day or so I was too ashamed to call her. I finally did phone her at her new boardinghouse. She wasn't in and the rather unpleasant landlady said she wouldn't take a message. She said, "They're supposed to get their own phones in their own rooms. I can't go keeping track of all their boyfriends." She added, "This is an approved university rooming house," and hung up.

The next week I was buried under work again, and Elizabeth Mary told me that she'd read what I'd done on my dissertation and wished to discuss it. That discussion and its aftermath took all my concentration. Elizabeth Mary thought it was pretty good, but wanted a larger sense of context in the introduction and something more vital by way of conclusion. She pointed out that it wasn't too late to go shopping for a better job if I got it done right away.

So it wasn't until a month had passed that I really missed Honorée's visits. And then I was reminded not by Honorée but by Miss Quist's dropping by during my evening office hours.

She was dressed in a business suit with a ruffled blouse and would have looked quite prim had she not been wearing shiny raspberry lipstick and matching nail polish. She'd been in class regularly but we hadn't spoken since her speech.

I asked her to sit down. She sat in silence for a moment. She looked forlorn, but I didn't trust her.

She said, "Is your officemate going to come in?"

I said she wasn't.

Miss Quist said, "I asked that because this is going to be really hard to say. I want to say I'm really sorry, I really didn't mean any harm, I just meant to tease Honorée a little and I didn't think anyone would get it except her because she'd talked about how much she liked you but just to me and I didn't think anyone else knew. I mean, it could have been some of the other girls. A lot of the girls think you're really neat. Kathy O'Rourke said she thought it might be her. You can ask her."

I had a clear memory of Miss Quist's and Miss O'Rourke's conversation by *Pioneer Woman.*

I said, "I'm sure Miss O'Rourke would back you up."

"Well, anyway, I just wanted to say that I'm really, really sorry. It was really dumb of me to fool around like that with Honorée's feelings. I know I was just trying to be funny, but I guess I'm just not any good at that kind of humor. So I'm going to apologize to Honorée and I just felt I should apologize to you too."

Miss Quist stood up. I stood up. She took my hand and shook it, saying, "There, I'm sorry." She put her left hand on top of our joined hands for emphasis.

I was surprised when she sat back down. She said, "Now, this part is just as hard. I'll tell you—my dad always told me never to ask for anything I hadn't earned by working for it. I really believe that. So here's what's bothering me a little. My sorority is going to put me up for homecoming queen next fall. Now, I probably won't make queen, but I might just make one of the princesses of the court. But the deal is this. I have to have a three point for the sorority to do it so that people don't think the homecoming queen election is just a beauty contest. So I was doing fine, I had a three point one for the fall, but now I may not. My big paper for your course only got a two five. So I thought maybe it was because you were upset over what we were just talking about—about Honorée and all."

I started to speak, but Miss Quist went on.

"I know you're fair and everything. And I wouldn't blame you for anything. I just wanted you to feel how important this is to me. I mean, I'll do it over, or I can do extra work, or anything you say."

I said, "I'll get another opinion. But I must warn you, if the grade comes back lower—"

"Oh, Mr. Hendricks—oh, that wouldn't work. It's *your* opinion. I'm not just asking you about the paper—it's all the work. I know I made a mistake and you have every right not to forgive me if that's the way you feel." She leaned forward in her chair, wringing her hands. I felt uncomfortable, but I knew I could resist her. I believed she was capable of the ridiculous cliché of offering her favors, in which case I thought I would ask her if that was what her dad had in mind when he'd told her to ask only for her due. I was prepared to be brutal.

Miss Quist said, "This is really more important to me than anything. One of the girls in the sorority told me a month ago that I had a chance but that one of the guys I was going out with had got into trouble by taking some stuff from the pharmacy department and I'd better not go with him anymore. She and another girl called me into their room in the sorority and asked me what I'd do. It was awful. They just sat there while I cried about it. And they just sat there until I said I wouldn't see him. I just cried all night."

Miss Quist looked up at me. She had moved herself to the brink of tears.

"So you see. It's not just . . ." She began to cry. She wiped her eyes with her fingers. She said, "I'm sorry. Don't pay any attention to this. I've got a hanky. Don't pay any attention to this." She got up and walked around the office, trying to catch her breath. She leaned forward against the wall. I stood up.

I said, "Miss Quist—"

"I know you don't like me," she said.

"Miss Quist—"

"But you don't understand." She turned around and walked up to me. She said furiously, "But I care this much."

I stepped back, afraid. But she wasn't looking at me. She turned the reflector of my gooseneck lamp up toward her and put her fingers on the burning bulb. I heard the dampness crisp off her fingers. She cried out, "Ow! Ow!" and put her other hand in her mouth.

I finally grabbed her by the shoulders and sat her back down in the chair. She held her burned hand by the wrist. I ran down the hall and brought back a cup of cold water. I took her wrist and put her fingers in the water.

I knelt there for some time; Miss Quist didn't move. I felt my assessment of her, my calculation, come unfastened and slide about, like loose cargo in the hold of a ship.

She finally said, "Here—I can hold that," and took the cup. I sat down again.

I took her theme from her folder. I read it over. It wasn't very good, but I'd given better grades to worse. I looked up her speech-grading blank. Her speech, from a technical point of view, had not been as bad as I had marked it. Voice, eye contact, unity of central theme—they could all be three point five. I looked at Miss Quist. I was helpless to know what was now sweetening her wheedling, hypocritical apology, her lying, her malice, her bad taste, "My dad always told me . . ."

She took her hand out of the water. There were three puffed-up blisters on her middle fingers.

I thought perhaps she wasn't Iago. She was Edmund. I thought of Edmund's soliloquy in *King Lear*—the wonderful fire of contempt for tepid legitimacy: "Now, gods, stand up for bastards!"

Was there any element—water, earth, air, or fire—that I could resist in women?

I said, "Miss Quist, in one sense you are in the right and I am in the wrong. This course we are pursuing is not a course in morals but in rhetoric—"

She quickly said, "That means you'll do it? Oh, that's so neat! I really will be better, you'll see. I always do better when I'm doing work for someone who really cares."

She made her exit, turning back just before she closed the door to compress her mouth, squint her eyes, and shimmy her face at me—a signal to express wriggling pleasure.

I wondered what I'd tell Honorée.

I finally ran into Honorée at the theater department's costume party.

Elizabeth Mary asked me to take her; she said we should really make an appearance. Elizabeth Mary went as a nun. Her face looked quite wonderful framed in a wimple. Her skin looked even more delicate and gold than usual: the texture appeared to be as smooth as a mushroom cap. Her eyes were only a slightly darker shade than her skin—really no darker than dark hazel.

She made me go as a monk in a baggy brown robe and

sandals. I felt very foolish, but at least the robe made it easy to cover up what passed as my dancing.

Honorée came as part of a Gay Nineties chorus line. They all wore net stockings and a sort of abbreviated velveteen costume with a ruffled skirt that was cut high across the thigh in front but had a flounce or bustle in the back. They came on as part of the entertainment and actually did a kick-and-prance number in the middle of the dance floor. Honorée was the shortest of the five and looked a little chunky by contrast. As soon as she left them, however, she looked adorable. She went to the edge of the dance floor and stood peering around the room. Her fine straight hair was fluffed up from her bouncing around and her pale face was glowing. She had a rather old-fashioned fullness of thigh, bust, and upper arm that went well with her costume. I was surprised and touched to see that much strong ripeness so intimately connected to her sweet girlish face. Her body seemed a part of her costume; her real self was in her look, a look of someone expecting to be surprised—her eyes wide, her lips ready to smile.

When she saw me, however, she blushed and closed her eyes.

She said, "Oh, God, I'm so embarrassed."

"I've been trying to get hold of you."

"Oh, Mr. Hendricks, I almost died in that class. It wasn't true, you know. I may have talked to her about things, but she made them seem as though I was, you know, *planning* things. Of course, it may have seemed that way to her, so she may not have been actually lying. And I may have said some things to her that weren't the way I felt just so that she wouldn't think I was completely dumb."

Honorée pulled the top of her bodice up with both hands and held them there, pressing them into her breastbone.

She said, "I know you understand it all, but I'm still embarrassed."

"Miss Quist told me she was going to apologize to you. Has she come to see you?"

"No. But I'm so hard to get hold of these days."

Elizabeth Mary came up. I introduced them.

Honorée told Elizabeth Mary that she was in her course and loved it. Elizabeth Mary thanked her.

Honorée said in a suddenly different tone, "It's an interesting sensation standing here with two of my teachers, wearing practically nothing but a bathing suit. But then, if we all went around like this all the time, it wouldn't feel odd at all."

Since neither Elizabeth Mary nor I could think of anything to say to that, Honorée was flustered. After a pause she said, "I often imagine the two of you in your office together. It must be so wonderful. Even when you're not talking, I imagine there must be a sort of humming between your minds. It must—"

"That would be most distracting, all that humming," Elizabeth Mary said. "I'm afraid you have quite a romantic view. We hardly talk at all when we happen to be there together. It's just work, work, work."

Elizabeth Mary then surprised me. She took Honorée's hand in hers and said, "We just work very hard so we can try to appear brilliant to you." She stroked Honorée's forearm, saying in a soothing voice, "Work, work, work."

Honorée thought about this. She said in a reflective way, "Oh. I guess you just can't imagine something until you already know what it's like."

Elizabeth Mary said, "No, no. There are some things one can only get right by imagining. But, Oliver, I must get home. I have more work to do. Miss Hogentogler, your dance was very good and you are a very charming creature in your costume, but we must say good night."

When Elizabeth Mary got into the car, she laughed. "Oh, Oliver, you are such a cruel creature. You should either do something with that smitten girl or stop smiting her. Really, she is wriggling like a fish on your line." She laughed again.

I said, "She'd take it very seriously."

"Oh, I think not. I think it could be over in no time at all with no hard feelings."

I said, "That really isn't possible with someone like Honorée. And for that matter, it may not be the sort of thing I'm capable of."

Elizabeth Mary said, "Don't tell me you believe in total love or nothing. Or perhaps that you believe someone of proper feeling only falls in love once. Ah! No wonder, then, you are so wedded to your Shakespeare. That's why you are so 'true to the age.' Really, Oliver, you are all of a piece."

I felt a little bullied. But it may have been because I was still too impressed by her training and knowledge. She hadn't yet told me what a hard early life she'd had, though I should have imagined that it would have been difficult for a girl of such mixed races to be at ease. I was under the impression that she was an example of George Bernard Shaw's theory of eugenics—the best mixture of several racial geniuses. And I'd also only recently learned that she'd begun her education in science and had actually started medical school when she switched fields. She was of course very well prepared linguistically for comparative literature—she spoke Portuguese from birth, English from early childhood. She was brought up a Roman Catholic at a time when Latin was still in use. Her mother's brother then sent her to school in Switzerland, where all her classes were in French. She also learned German. She worked for a year or two as a secretary in Switzerland, then quite bravely set out for America to go to college. This dossier of bright achievement was foremost in my mind, but I should have imagined there were shadows.

Of course, I was also under the spell of her sharp beauty, but in such a way that it made me cross. I thought her attractive, even desirable, but not sexual—at least not without refracting her attraction and desirability through some prism of grotesque fantasy. Perhaps it was the temptation of this fantasy that made me cross.

Or perhaps it was because she was capable of maintaining her own privacy while invading mine. She could send a flicker of attention into my state of mind that gave me an eerie feeling of being possessed.

At this moment, her teasing me about Honorée had yet another annoyance: that she could hover benignly over a pastoral interlude, the outline of which was clear to her as it was not to Honorée, and as it would not be to me unless she offered me her view of it.

She said, "Now I've made you angry, Oliver. I only meant to chaff you up a bit."

I said, "You know, I sometimes worry that a theorist like you may know the structure of everything and the essence of nothing."

She laughed. "Oh, well replied! You've run me right through. Well adapted, dear Oliver."

All her talk then became a light caressing of my mood—a wonderfully pleasant sensation—but after I dropped her off at her apartment I felt restless.

Elizabeth Mary was certainly a friend, practically my only immediate friend, but still not a comfortable friend.

The next day Elizabeth Mary and I went out for coffee. While we were sitting at a table we saw, through the plate-glass window, Honorée and a young man wearing bib overalls and an Amish hat. They didn't see us. Elizabeth Mary said, "That boy with Miss Hogentogler is in my graduate seminar. He wanted to submit a short film in place of one of his papers. He was quite cross when I said no."

I supposed he was the director of Honorée's movie. I asked, "Is he smart?"

"Not in any useful way for the seminar. He has a cleverness that was quite impressive at first, but now I see how it works, I'm dissatisfied. Its main device is an *esprit de contradiction*. He'll say things like 'Romeo and Juliet didn't really like each other very much.' It's all to astonish. But I did like one of his short films. It was quite witty in a visual way; also quite pretty. He will present some more at the Spring Arts Festival."

I had heard of the Spring Arts Festival. In fact, it was in connection with it that I first heard the word "counterculture." I at first thought it was a synonym of "anti-intellectual." Elizabeth Mary started off being sharp with the first local counterculture yearnings for Eastern enlightenment. She told the students who came to talk to her about Indian thought that it was too tedious to discuss it with them, and they were much better off studying the writers in her course. But she was more alert than I was to the phenomenon as a whole. To her credit it must be said that she clearly perceived the elements that were vigorous and contagious. She got me to pay attention, and the two of us attended a number of events that I might not have thought any more important or coherent than the usual student spring assertions.

The "guerrilla theater" was crude but curiously successful. The sketch—it wasn't really a play—was called "Equal Time." The theater department hadn't approved it, so it was put on in a circus tent in a field just outside town. It was a parody of a 4-H Club exposition. There was a master of ceremonies who gave prizes for the best pies—the supposed cooks got into a quarrel and threw the pies in each other's faces. Predictable slapstick. The ringmaster announced prizes for the best marijuana plants. At this point someone in the audience got up to protest. It was prearranged. The ringmaster blew his whistle and said, "All right! All right! Equal time! Equal time for decency and normality!"

A group of girls brought on classroom chairs with writing

arms attached. A woman wearing a gray wig with a bun came on with a tripod holding a series of large posters. She carried a pointer. The first poster announced "Sexual Hygiene 101."

The lecturer's voice was pained and nasal.

"Now, girls, it's better you learn these things here than in the gutter."

The ringmaster wandered among the girls, who pretended not to see him. He mugged ferociously.

The lecturer turned the first display card: "Death Before Dishonor—The Case for Virginity."

The lecturer said, "Now, girls, how can he respect you if you haven't saved yourself for him?"

A girl raised her hand and wailed, "But suppose it's too late? I have a friend and she—"

The ringmaster rolled his eyes and the audience laughed.

Another girl said, "Maybe she could lie about it."

The lecturer said, "Lying isn't right, girls, but there are ways to avoid undue references to premarital experiences. And there are ways to properly refer to them if references are necessary."

The girl said, "Oh, I've got some great references."

The ringmaster went down on his hands and knees and pointed at her like a bird dog.

"It's still mass taste," I said to Elizabeth Mary.

"But it's a burlesque of the forces in their lives," Elizabeth Mary said.

"It's not burlesque, it's burleycue."

The next day Elizabeth Mary didn't feel well, so I set off by myself for the student union, where the films were being shown.

The small theater was full and I was about to go away when Honorée stopped me.

"Do you want to see the films, Mr. Hendricks? Come with me."

She took me to the projection booth with a pretty air of

authority. Someone inside recognized her and let us in. "O.K.," she said to me. "Climb aboard."

These backstage airs charmed me. Of course, they were for my benefit, but even so, I felt a sympathy for her vanity and excitement.

I asked her if this was the movie she was in.

She said, "Oh, no; that's not finished yet. These are just some of Phil's exercises. There may be one at the end that has me in it." She asked the projectionist, "What do we have of Phil's?"

I thought: My little girl in show biz.

Honorée couldn't sit still through the first short piece. She wriggled and whispered so that I barely saw it. When there was applause she grabbed my arm for joy.

The second was silly but amusing. A pastiche of spy films in which every third shot was a jet plane landing and then a postcard-like shot of the Eiffel Tower or palm trees or the Manhattan skyline. There would be one scene played in a room in which several people explained things in rapid-fire dialogue made up of comic book clichés. Then all the actors would rush to the window to watch a car blow up. It was always the same car. Then the jet plane taking off and landing and another establishing shot.

The last piece came closest to being real work. It was called "Pibroch." There was no narrative. Image followed image; the only link I could think of was that in most cases whatever was being photographed was seen in such a way that it was unrecognizable at first. The screen would fill with what seemed a washed-out afterimage of the previous shot—for example, an apple falling into halves as it was cut, seen from only a few inches away—but the new picture developed into, or turned out to be, the top sheet of a bed being pulled down, viewed obliquely so that the slight shadow between the top and bottom sheets appeared at first to be the knife edge still severing two whitenesses. Then this shot was shown in negative, and gradually darkened. When it lightened again one realized that the new picture was of a white churning line (the wake of a motor-boat?) dividing two masses of dark water, seen from directly above. And finally, in that sequence, lips parting.

Honorée giggled and I recognized the mouth as hers.

All the images came again at a faster pace and with an occasional hop backward—apple, sheets, negative sheets, apple, negative sheets, water—which gave the effect of an added grace note.

At its best, the film did have a compelling visual rhythm. And a number of the pictures were beautiful in themselves. But they were always being mastered by tricks. Of course, a great deal of Elizabethan poetry is neat tricks—quibbles and con-ceits—but I couldn't overcome a slight rankling.

Honorée and I went outside during intermission. Some people were flying kites on the playing field in front of the student union. Honorée gazed up at the kites and then shut her eyes.

I asked her if she was all right.

"Oh, yes. I'm just a little dazed these days. I don't think anything's wrong."

"What do you mean? You aren't—you haven't taken up drugs, have you?"

"Oh, no," she said. "I had an affair, but that didn't do anything. I mean, it didn't mean anything. It was really"—she shrugged her shoulders and looked airily away up the slope—"just an affair I got bored with." She laughed and then once more stared at my face for a sign, her gaze sweeping back and forth from one of my eyes to the other.

I wasn't really surprised. I did think of how far it was from "Our dog is named Kartoffel" to "It was really just an affair I got bored with," just as a matter of diction.

"You don't think that I shouldn't—I mean, you don't think it's shocking that I got bored?"

"No," I said. "Sooner or later, I guess. I mean, having an affair."

"That's just what I thought."

I said, "Do you—I mean, I assume you use . . ." She nodded her head quickly. It made her hair bounce along her cheeks.

"Well, don't take any drugs," I said. "Marijuana may be all right, but . . ."

"All right," she said. She took my hand. "I'm glad you're here. Did you think his film was good? It really is good, don't you think?"

"It really is very good," I said. "It really is."

"Well, I'm glad you're here. Will you come tomorrow? We're going to shoot the last scene." Honorée laughed. "I get assumed into heaven."

"What?"

"Oh, it's sort of silly in a way. It's a kind of Marx Brothers version of the gospel, and some other Catholic dogma. Phil was a Catholic and—oh, it's too complicated to tell you the plot except that the apostles are sort of Keystone Kops and the Virgin Mary is really smart. Sort of like Snow White with the seven dwarfs."

"Are you the Virgin Mary?"

Honorée said, "No. I'm Mary Magdalene. But in this version I'm really good."

I said, "In the original, Mary Magdalene is good."

"Well, yes—but in this I'm innocent. I mean, it's good to make love and so no one minds except—oh, it's too complicated. You'll have to see it. I shouldn't have tried to explain it. A lot of my part is just being chased by the apostles. In this I like men O.K., but I can't stand beards, so I run away. When they finally catch me I turn into an angel and fly away. I know it sounds silly, but anyway it's all over except that last part tomorrow, so there's no point in worrying about it. They've all been just wonderful."

All the while she was talking she held my hand. At first I thought I was embarrassed to be seen this way in the middle of the campus, but then I realized it was something else that bothered me—some sense of Honorée's endless possibility of feeling and the small speck she actually now made on the surface of her life.

That evening I visited Elizabeth Mary in the hospital. She was under observation, since she'd had some dizzy spells.

She said, "Oliver, do you know what I think? I think I have actually got the vapors. The doctor is quite cross with me, as I won't be a good little girl. I have just enough medical knowledge to know he's completely at sea. I tell him not to be embarrassed that he doesn't know, and that makes him even more cross with me."

She gave me a list of little errands to do—I was to distribute various materials to her students and tell them to go to a lecture in another course if she wasn't out of the hospital by Tuesday.

I felt very odd myself. I couldn't tell if I felt more like Elizabeth Mary or more like her doctor. Some question was moving through my mind, troubling me by not taking form, by being at the wrong distance. The physical symptoms were exactly those of immediate embarrassment—a hot prickling stuffiness in my thought. But there wasn't the cold internal condensing of shame that usually followed.

The next morning I thought it might just be the weather, which was both muggy and gusty. I had hoped for a sharp spring day, but the atmosphere was blurred. As I was about to leave my house, a bird flew under the porch roof and hit the front window. I was startled, then reassured that there *was* something wrong with the day if a bird could be so off kilter. The bird recovered and flew off, bobbing through the air in an unbroken line of Palmer penmanship *i*'s.

I wondered if there was a technical name for fear of spring. Honorée had told me that her group would be in costume for the parade—one of the events of the festival, a parody of the football-weekend "homecoming" that Miss Quist was looking forward to. After the parade they would drive off with their pickup and wagon full of gear to do their scene.

In town the sidewalks were lined with people. The same little boys who sold Hawkeye pennants and black-and-gold pompons were selling balloons with "Love" on them.

And at first it was the duplication I noticed more than the parody. There was an Indian—that is, someone dressed as an Indian—in full feathers riding in front of a small brass band that played "Hail to the Chief." There was a cowgirl on a pony, followed by a group carrying placards saying "Linda Zeckendorff for Sheriff." Her calves bulged prettily out of her boot tops as she pressed her pony from one side of the street to the other.

There were several floats and another brass band. One thing I noticed about the Midwest—brass bands are easy to come by. I think it may be the German tradition. Almost all the children learn to tootle along on some kind of horn.

There was a float mocking the student health service—a patient swathed in red tape. Various bandaged students carrying crutches struggled to climb aboard and were beaten away by a nurse and a doctor holding huge plastic thermometers. As far as I could see, it was the style and wit of the Beat Purdue floats of the fall.

Following that there was a man on a bicycle decked out with American flags. He was a figure about town—a harmless sparse-haired fellow who wandered about on his fat-wheel Schwinn with a large basket, picking through the trash baskets behind the stores. He was meant to represent the motorcycle escort for the homecoming queen, who followed in a convertible. She was in fact a store-window mannequin with a blond wig. She—or it—wore a large silver cape which had a phone number in orange Day-Glo numerals on the back.

Honorée's group came next. The twelve apostles were in

harness, pulling a farm wagon. They all had grotesquely long false beards. In the wagon was a large globe, on top of which sat the Virgin Mary, in a blue robe over a white gown. She had a halo of stars. Honorée, who was behind her, helped her to stand up on the globe and arranged a large rubber serpent under her feet. There was some laughter at this; I was surprised at first that so many people recognized this emblem. Then I thought it was simply that everyone was having a good time. I was envious for a moment. Were their sources of unhappiness so easily dealt with?

Honorée saw me, and we waved to each other. She was wearing a metallic halo like a hat brim without a crown. It was tilted back so that it shone around her face. She pointed with her free hand behind the wagon to a pickup truck. Rising out the bed of the pickup was a partly inflated balloon. She pointed to herself and then pointed up. I suddenly caught her mood. It was a kind of glee that was almost too sweet, almost too large. It seemed to burst behind my senses, pressing them into a fever.

I went back to my car and down out of town to the field where the "guerrilla theater" had been and where Honorée's group would now shoot their scene.

The pickup truck arrived with the balloon, compression tanks, and valves, and the wagon full of apostles, Virgin Mary, and Honorée. Another station wagon followed, with the director, two cameramen, cameras, and tripods. Then another car, with several more people and mechanical devices. The entire caravan lumbered up a grassy slope to a barn.

It took a half hour before they stopped milling about. Honorée was being fussed over in the barn. She finally emerged. Her dress was now a Roman gown of soft muslin held up by ribbons tied across her bare shoulders and loosely belted below the bust. She eyed the balloon, which was now fully inflated. Suspended from the shrouds there was, instead of a basket, a device that looked like the seat of an infant's swing, called, I later learned, a bosun's chair.

There was a burst of activity. The crowd of assistants cleared away, and Honorée and the apostles came running up the hill. The director began to instruct them through a bullhorn. The apostles surrounded Honorée. The director said, "Fog! Now the fog!"

A machine spewed out a pinkish fog around the swarm of actors. The camera seemed to stop every ten or fifteen seconds. At last all of them regrouped under the balloon. The Virgin Mary came out and fitted a pair of huge wings over Honorée's arms. They were fully feathered on both sides—Honorée's arm went inside the envelope of feathered material through several rubber rings.

Then the fog again, as the apostles began to swarm around and then on top of Honorée. But then she was suddenly lifted up in the balloon seat as the apostles clasped her about the knees and ankles. Her dress slithered down in several pieces. Honorée rose another yard, her wings crossed in front of her. The director said, "Blinding light!" and several spotlights mounted on the truck began to dart their beams into the fog. "Higher!" Honorée rose again above the lifted arms of the apostles. "Fly!" Honorée leaned forward against the seat belt and, lifting her face, uncrossed her arms and spread her wings.

"Apostles, consternation!" The apostles began to fall to the ground.

"O.K., move her toward the barn camera."

The man holding the line attached to the balloon seat began to walk toward the barn.

"Flap your wings!"

Honorée's bare bosom had somehow not been surprising until then. She'd looked like the figurehead of a sailing ship—her face blank and thrust forward, her shoulders flexed back so that her collarbone, bust, and rib cage were a compound curve carved out of a single block. But as she began to flap her wings she became flesh. Honorée's legs, emerging in a straight line below the bosun's chair, were firmly held together, her toes pointed, as though she were diving forward.

She passed directly over my head on her way to the barn. At every flap I could see the movement of the muscles in her shoulders and stomach. Her joined legs moved in a sort of dolphin kick. Each slow downward beat of her wings seemed to lift her upper body slightly.

The director shouted encouragement. The two boys holding the cameraman on the barn roof cheered.

The balloon hovered over the barn, twenty feet above Honorée on its long shrouds. There was some confusion as the man holding the line reached the barn. Honorée's feet touched the barn roof. One of the boys holding the cameraman moved to grab her, but the balloon sailed past. Honorée seemed to leap into the air off the other side. She sailed free, the line to the ground sliding past the cameraman, who grabbed for it with one hand, holding one leg of the camera tripod with the other.

She swung from side to side very slowly as the balloon moved away. The director shouted through the bullhorn, "Pull up the line! Don't let the line hit a wire! Pull it up!" Then he got in the back of the pickup and thumped on the roof of the cab. The driver started off, but then the director stopped him to pick up a camera and tripod.

They got to the fence at the bottom of the field just as Honorée passed over it, but the balloon had stayed at the same height and the fence line was in a hollow.

The wind was not steady, but the gusts moved the balloon at a smooth pace, as though it was a paper boat gliding down a bubbling stream.

I got in my car and drove out the gate. The balloon didn't seem to be very high, but it wasn't coming down. One problem of getting under it in a car was that almost all the roads ran either north-south or east-west, and the wind now was out of the northwest, so that Honorée was crossing the fields diagonally while we had to drive at right angles, like rooks on a chessboard. The other problem was that we had to detour at first, as the roads crossing Interstate 80 were far apart.

The pickup truck crossed the overpass right behind me, but we diverged just after that. I headed south and they turned east. I turned east after two miles and at the next intersection we almost collided. I now had to keep an eye on the plume of dust they threw up as well as watch Honorée.

I got east of her after another two fields, and I stopped at what I hoped would be the point she crossed the dirt road. She had shaken one wing off in order to gather up the line with her hand, but she had her eye on the pickup truck, which was beyond me to the southeast. I yelled to her to drop the line, but it fell too far away. As I ran up to it, it slithered across the fence. She gathered it back up. She had not only shed her right wing but had somehow punched her left hand through the material of her left wing.

She crossed the corner of the field. The director was running the camera in the bed of the pickup. When she drew near, it was clear she would pass astern of the truck. He yelled to the driver to back up. The driver overshot the line, which flapped past the windshield.

A new problem presented itself. The balloon was now passing just east of my house and toward the Iowa River. I knew there was no road across the river for several miles. Where the balloon would cross the river the bank was lined with tall oak trees. The river itself ran more or less to the east-southeast, so the balloon was only slowly angling toward it. I drove onto the first bridge. I saw the pickup hurtle past the turn to the bridge, a half mile away.

I now saw the balloon, still on the north side of the river. I backed off the bridge and followed it. The balloon crossed in front of the truck. Honorée held the coil of rope in her hands as she drifted over the telephone lines. She dropped it in the field beside the road. Both the director and the cameraman climbed the wire fence and ran after it, but it slithered over another fence before they could reach it. They turned around and ran back to their truck.

I drove back to the bridge, crossed it, and drove downstream. The balloon was now over the oak trees on the north side of the river. I was relieved at this. There were no power lines for a good distance on either side of the river. I was driving slowly now, since I'd got ahead of the balloon. The pickup passed me and turned toward the river on a farmer's road. They opened the gate and passed through. I thought perhaps they knew of a bridge, so I started to follow them. The dirt road turned into a grassy lane as it entered the woods. The pickup jounced several times and then stopped. As I drew closer I saw that the rear wheels were spinning in a deep puddle between the roots of an oak tree.

The director jumped out of the pickup bed and ran toward me. I would have let him in if he hadn't been carrying his camera, which he'd unscrewed from the tripod. I backed away. He chased me all the way to the road. I backed onto it. As I started forward, he jumped on the hood. His rear end made a dent in it, but he slid off to one side.

I drove down the road to the next turn toward the river and reached a one-lane bridge. The balloon, sailing over midstream, was now much lower. (Honorée later explained to me that the air was cooler over the water, and this created a downdraft.) Honorée lowered the rope when she was a hundred yards upstream. It splashed into the water in a coil. The rope seemed to act as a sea anchor for a moment. I ran one way and then the other, unsure of where the line would drag across the bridge. I then was afraid the line might drag over the girders at the midpoint and be out of reach. I climbed up on the downstream girder, which was wide enough to stand on. Honorée floated toward me. I moved a step to the left. The balloon, then Honorée, passed over the upstream girder, the rope trailing behind her. She reached down with her wing, and I grabbed it.

She spun into me, and I started to fall. I grabbed her around the hips, and she grabbed the shoulder of my jacket with her free hand. We balanced for an instant. Honorée swung her knees up under my armpits and held on to me with her legs. We toppled slowly at first, then plunged into the water. My face pressed into her stomach as we splashed. I felt a second of terror. I let go, but she was still holding me in a scissors grip. I suddenly relaxed since we seemed to be floating up, and since Honorée, from the movements of her body as they reached me, appeared to be paddling with her arms—or rather with an arm and a wing.

In another instant we were at the surface, moving downstream in the smooth muddy current. The balloon was floating ahead of us, slightly collapsed. Honorée was trying to undo the strap of her bosun's chair. I thought it would be better to get to shore first, so I swam, pulling two of the shrouds. We were by now a hundred yards downstream of the bridge, entering a curve of the river. The balloon floated into the branches of a tree leaning over the water. The webbing around it snagged, and we drifted by, as though we were skaters at the end of a snap-the-whip line. Honorée floated on her back, held in place by the taut shrouds and her chair. We'd been swung in toward shore, so I could now touch bottom, though the water was up to my shoulders. Honorée held me in place against the current while I unbuckled the canvas strap around her waist. She slid out of the chair and bumped into me again, as she had on top of the bridge. We turned once and I swung her toward the steep mud bank, which she grabbed by plunging her fingers in, up to the first joint. It was very hard to move, and I realized I was terribly cold. Our mouths were drawn so tight that neither of us could speak for a moment. We crawled up the crumbling bank, dislodging black clods. We reached the top and lay full length in the green weeds.

Honorée was shivering. I took off my jacket and held it

out for her. She raised herself on her elbows and said, "I'm too stiff to move. I can barely talk." She rubbed her mouth and jaw with one hand.

I got to my knees and floundered around to her other side to pull off her wing. Struggling with the wing revived us both. She sat up and I handed her my jacket. She got to her knees and wrung it out. There was something so domestic about the gesture that it was even more modest than if she'd put it on. She squeezed the water out of the loose hem of her gym shorts too. She put the jacket on. It covered her shorts, right down to the Wapsi Valley High School insignia. She rolled the jacket sleeves up and lifted her hair from inside the neck.

Honorée said, "Mr. Hendricks, your mouth is blue."

I said, "Honorée, you're wonderful. You are a heroine. You are a—"

"Oh, shsh," she said. "Oh, just hush." I didn't understand. She didn't say it crossly. I felt exhilarated inside my daze. In fact, we were both dazed. I felt the sphere of my attention condense around us, as though we were in a grove of feelings, flowering to celebrate Honorée's rich, thick body. She was innocent of its fact, of its appeal. The disconnection between her submissive fondness for me and her suddenly triumphant beauty was wonderfully mysterious. But the beauty itself was even more mysterious: all that I knew about other women's beauty was now chaos, and her sweet chunkiness became the only true form.

This mystery and excitement seemed to hold me immobile and timeless, and my sensation was one of power. It lasted until I heard the pickup truck drive onto the bridge.

Honorée laughed and raised me up—I had fallen to my knees and embraced her lower half, pressing myself against the perfect ovals of her knees, and against the plump swelling of thigh muscle. I hugged the firm square of her hips and buttocks, two full volumes tightly shelved.

Let it stand. I recognized then and there the absurd mixing of genres. For the instant it was an amazing liberty.

Honorée and I picked our way through the brush to the road. The director and his cameraman were standing behind my car. They were relieved to see Honorée unharmed, but they immediately asked us to help them retrieve the balloon. I said we were too cold and wet to help. Honorée and I got in my car and drove off.

We drove through the countryside. We grew steamy in the blast of the car heater. It was dusk. We passed a farmhouse. Honorée said it looked like her house. Its clean white porch was lit by a simple yellow "no-bug" light. It suggested a cell, not one in a jail or an asylum, but a chamber in which to be subject to visions. This chamber of artificial light stood against the dark house and the darkening violet sky, the bare bulb standing in for the missing moon.

Honorée said, "Why can't every day be like today?" She paused. "It *could* be."

"Weren't you frightened?"

"No; not too bad except once or twice," she said. "I was more excited. . . . I could see for miles. I don't mean that I want everything to be *that* exciting all the time. I just mean— oh, I don't know exactly."

I realized her ecstasy had been impersonal—that when I'd called her a heroine she'd been beyond praise of herself. That was why she'd hushed me.

"I was going to untie myself even if they hadn't let me go. Once I got up I didn't want to just be pulled down."

"Weren't you embarrassed?"

"Oh, no. We'd done, you know, scenes like that before. It doesn't matter so much what you do if it's for a part; you don't mind if the *character* does things, because that's not you. You can even look ugly or stupid and not mind." She added with a sudden brightness, "Otherwise actors wouldn't ever play villains."

"Oh, Honorée," I said.

"Isn't that right, Mr. Hendricks? Or are you thinking about

something else? Wasn't today pretty good for you too? Was it interesting? I mean, maybe this thing will be a really good film. I feel that there is that possibility. We don't have to be geniuses to just be good. I really felt I was in the middle of something." Honorée stretched her toes toward the heater. She put her hands under her legs to hold them off the seat. I stopped the car at an intersection. I wasn't sure where we were.

Honorée said, "Go left. Town's somewhere that way." She continued. "I can't tell what you're thinking. I used to think I could but now I can't. Of course, maybe when you get closer to someone, they get blurred."

I felt myself almost coaxed into simplicity, but I foresaw that it would be an impersonation. The immediate counter-stroke, unfortunately, was that I saw the care and patience of my habitual frame of mind as contrivance. I thought—although only for a short while—that I might be keeping accounts for a phantom enterprise, that Elizabeth Mary was right in saying that there was no true center to any age or culture, and that there was therefore nothing but one's own adventure, one's own passage through human thought, which was as trackless, formless, and all-receiving as the sea.

One would always find America and not the Indies. And one could never return to the mother country—the mother country was as chimerical as the Indies. Only adventure. I hated that idea. I'd thought that was Elizabeth Mary's existential contrivance to keep her own courage up.

I thought of Feste the jester, speaking to the Duke: ". . . for thy mind is a very opal! I would have men of such constancy put to sea, that their business might be everything, and their intent everywhere; for that's it that always makes a good voyage of nothing."

When we got to the edge of town, Honorée said she'd prefer to go to my house since I had a bathtub, and her place only had a shower. When we got to my house she became silly, and not very funny. All my exuberance had waned, and I could tell she was disappointed in me. But she kept on pushing, as though she had to make absolutely sure I was not everything she'd thought me. I recognized the grim determination to wreck an idol. I'd felt the same urge when faced with cousin Josie's foolish backing away.

Honorée kept saying, "Come on—just be yourself." In nervous reaction to this slogan, I found myself spewing bits of quotations. She thought I was doing this as a joke, as a caricature of my own manner. I discovered that she became nervous in the face of detailed praise of her looks. I couldn't help persisting in it. She finally said, "Look, I've had to talk about my elbows, my nose, my everything with all those guys. So it's not so much fun. And I don't really believe it. No, I believe it sort of, but it feels like I'm being teased."

She added later, "You never say things to Miss Chetty about her looks. She's too beautiful."

She burned her hand cooking supper. I said to put butter on it, and she contradicted me flatly. By the time we finally embraced, we'd both been cross and we were both grieved. I'm not sure what her awareness of her feelings actually was, but I sensed that she was still toppling her idea of me.

Much later that night, just as I was falling asleep, Honorée said, "Oliver, now I am embarrassed." I think she meant she was sorry, but I was too thinly there to respond.

I don't remember our several subsequent meetings. I do remember going to see Elizabeth Mary the day after the balloon ascension. That was when she told me she thought she'd had a stroke. The doctors had told her there was no evidence of it. Elizabeth Mary said she had two clear symptoms. One was a slight stutter that occurred occasionally and unpredictably. The other symptom was that on one occasion she hadn't been able to add numbers. She'd been playing a card game by herself that required adding up the numbers of little piles of cards. She'd tried and tried but found that she couldn't even add, say, four and seven. She said that she knew the words for numbers but couldn't *see* their numerical value. She wished the doctor to consider whether this might be at least a symptom of transitory cerebral ischemia. The doctor had said he was considering every possibility and that she should stop arguing with him because that seemed to make her restless and that she needed rest.

Elizabeth Mary had first noticed her stammer when she had five of her seminar students in to see her. She said she was now terrified of giving a lecture. She had only four left before review week (what we used to call reading period). She wished the doctor to send for a speech pathologist. She knew that the University of Iowa had a very advanced speech pathology center. The doctor had said he'd look into it.

I tracked down Elizabeth Mary's doctor. At first he wouldn't talk to me, but finally I prevailed on him. What he told me, and what she hadn't told me, was that he had tentatively diagnosed her problem as an anxiety attack. He thought her dizzy spells came from hyperventilating, and that her hyperventilating was caused by anxiety.

I said, somewhat stupidly, "You mean it's just nerves?"

He explained, obviously not for the first time, "No, not *just* nerves. No, not *just* in her mind. Her symptoms are real, whatever their origin. Anxiety is not *just* a cop-out diagnosis on my part. The only thing I'm copping out on is prognosis. My guess is she'll feel better when she feels better. Sounds pretty dumb, huh? I gave her the name of a psychiatrist." I must have looked alarmed. He said, "That doesn't mean anything dramatic. It just means I've ruled out the possibilities that might have required the kind of treatment I'm competent at. O.K.? If I'm brusque with you, it doesn't mean I'm brusque with the patient. And finally, I think she's better—that is, I think her symptoms have abated. I've got to go now." He got up and added, "Look.

I'm sorry. I know you're a friend of hers. O.K.? That's a help. O.K.?"

I was still at a loss. When I saw Elizabeth Mary again, I asked if she'd recovered her use of numbers. She said she thought she had and asked me to check the grade point averages of her graduate seminar. I did. It only took several minutes. I said she'd got all fifteen of them right.

Elizabeth Mary asked about my own state of mind. I said I thought I was O.K. I told her about my spell of agoraphobia, and said that it hadn't recurred. I said that I'd just taken a drive through the countryside and had found it beautiful.

"Well, Oliver, that is reassuring, because you and I are birds of a feather. But I think I need an antidotal calming influence. I think I shall call Bobby and have him come visit me. Bobby is so untroubled, he is just what I need after being in hospital."

I said that was a good idea. I also said that she looked better. In fact, she looked quite beautiful, but frail. Her pale gold skin was drawn tight across her face. There was a shadow under her eyes.

She said, "Well, I shall just give my lectures. What is the worst that can happen? A hundred people I shall never see again will hear me sounding foolish. But I wish to see a speech therapist—I'm sure there are one or two little tricks that will help."

Bobby did fly out. I picked him up at the airport. It was wonderful to see him, and he was wonderful with Elizabeth Mary. We all drove to her lecture together. His presence made it a different occasion—he radiated cheerfulness, as though this trip was the biggest treat in the world and Elizabeth Mary's lecture a chance to catch up on something he'd always wanted to know about. He had acquired something of the charm his father had had in his prime—a steady flow of alert but slightly inarticulate enthusiasm for other people's events. I remember

feeling pleased by (but superior to) Mr. Morse's pleasure at
school functions, to which other fathers came looking tired and
bothered, or else alertly scanned the boys, inspecting us early
for traces of family faults. Mr. Morse liked the buildings, the
view, the glee club, the art room, the prospect of eating a meal
at the town inn, of being with us. And here it all was again—
Bobby at thirty saying how healthy the students looked, how
handsome the old stone capital, how much fun it was to come
out to see us.

"I'll bet Oliver knows a good place to eat lunch. What was
that ad we saw—the Amana Colonies? What about that?"

I said I didn't know; I'd heard of a German restaurant
there; it was quite a drive.

Elizabeth Mary said, "Bobby wants to see the countryside.
We shall all go. Do you know they have pigs here that are
entirely black to their waist and then entirely white? Or is it the
other way around?"

We arrived at the lecture hall. "A pig's waist?" Bobby said.
"Where on earth is a pig's waist?"

Elizabeth Mary said, "The same place as on a fish."

The transfusion of Bobby's good spirits into Elizabeth
Mary seemed to do the job.

She stood boldly at the podium, she apologized to the class
for having missed last Thursday's lecture, and then launched
into her topic with aplomb.

Honorée came in late and sat in the aisle beside Bobby
and me. I offered her my seat but she said no.

Elizabeth Mary faltered only two or three times; she got
past her difficulty in each case by almost singing the word and
then blending this note back into speech by half chanting the
next several words.

I was sympathetically exhausted by the end of the hour, so
I expected Elizabeth Mary to be near collapse, but when she
joined Bobby and me she was buzzing with energy. There was

a swirl of students about her in the aisle. Bobby looked at Elizabeth Mary's fans with interest and pleasure as he stood beside her. As the students began to leave, Honorée touched my arm. I'd lost track of her for the moment.

Elizabeth Mary said, "Bobby, I'm ravenous. Are you ready, Oliver?"

Bobby said to me, "Are you as good as she is? Don't tell me I'm the only dumb one in our gang." As he spoke he took in Honorée and smiled at her. Honorée smiled back. I introduced them.

Honorée laughed and said, "I know—you're Oliver's friend from school. It's so funny to see you like this because I think of you as a schoolboy. I mean, I heard about you as Oliver's roommate in boarding school. So I think of you as younger than me even though Oliver is older now."

Honorée became embarrassed. Bobby laughed and fussed over her. "Oh, no, no, no. He's probably told you all sorts of things, hasn't he? I can't stand it. Look—I'm not like he says. What did he say? I'll bet it was his other roommate." He held her wrist in a friendly way for a second, then clasped his hands together in comic pleading. Honorée squeezed her lips shut and tucked her chin in with pleasure. Bobby nodded at me and said, "Are you in this joker's class? Herr Professor here. Is he any good?" Honorée was smiling like a very young child being entertained by a teasing uncle.

The upshot was that Bobby invited Honorée to join us for lunch.

In a way that I didn't understand at the time, I felt diminished.

We had a huge German meal—sauerbraten and spaetzle—that made us sink into our chairs. Honorée and Bobby had chocolate cake with nuts in it. Elizabeth Mary was not, as I'd first feared, mad at Bobby for inviting Honorée. And Honorée wasn't shy or overeager. I finally realized the difficulty was all with me.

Honorée got Elizabeth Mary to tell the outline of her life. Honorée said that this confirmed her belief that she herself should travel more, have more adventures, and be more open to change. She hoped that by doing that she might become more like Elizabeth Mary.

Elizabeth Mary smiled at this compliment. I thought that Honorée sounded like Walt Whitman, all aggressive innocence.

Honorée asked Elizabeth Mary if it would be a good idea for her to go to Sweden for a year. Honorée said she probably would learn Swedish very fast since her mother had spoken it to her when she was a baby.

I said, "Saying 'Dere's a yady with a yight' when you're two years old isn't the same thing as speaking Swedish."

Bobby asked Honorée what "yady with a yight" was all about. Honorée told the story. Bobby loved it. He repeated, "Dere's *anudder* yady with a yight!" several times.

Honorée said, "If I went to Sweden and learned Swedish, then I might even try to be in a Swedish movie. Maybe not with Ingmar Bergman, but maybe with someone like him when he was just starting out."

"Or you could go sit at a drugstore counter at Hollywood and Vine," I said, "saying 'Dere's a yady with a yight,' to distinguish you from the other ten thousand apple-cheeked farm girls wearing too much make-up. Your dreaming is taking a bad turn. At least Miss Quist only wants to be homecoming queen. You used to wish for something better than movies."

Honorée turned to me and said seriously and much too slowly, "Why are you being so mean to me?"

I was stunned. Her saying that was out of the question; by the expression on her face she showed everyone she was wounded.

I said, "Honorée, don't be so touchy. For heaven sakes . . ." I was horribly embarrassed. I also felt a poisonous rage. There was a silence.

Elizabeth Mary said, "Honorée dear, sometimes boys will be nothing but boys. He teases you because he likes you."

Bobby said, " 'Boys will be nothing but boys.' That's really better. I like that better—'nothing but.' Pretty soon you'll be nothing but adorable. I was at a party once and a tall woman came up to me, a complete stranger, and she pinched my cheek and said, 'When God made you, sonny, he made you cute!' I can't tell you how charming it was. It may not sound as charming as it really was. But it was. So I drink to charm." He raised his glass to Elizabeth Mary and then to Honorée. He said to me, "Your problem is that you're resisting charm." He laughed. "And my problem is that I can't."

I said, "You remind me of your father when I first met him."

Bobby kept on entertaining everyone. I looked out the window. Bobby was very nice, and he was certainly my friend, but he was wrong about my resisting charm. He couldn't tell his own charm apart from what charmed him. I didn't resist what charmed me—I only wished to separate it from its impurities. Bobby was easily pleased and easily pleasant. He would have been corny if he hadn't been graceful.

But the main circumstance for me then was that Honorée had hurt my feelings worse than I'd hurt hers. I couldn't tell when. Perhaps it was her talk of wanting to change, to have adventures. All this talk of change and adventure made me wish for stillness, made me wish that accidents would vanish, that what was beautiful would be itself and nothing else.

And, as in a fairy tale, I got my wish. We all got our wishes. That is to say, we got to go on wishing. My wish became my seal.

Honorée ate the last crumbs of her cake there, finished the school year, and arranged to go to Sweden for the summer to stay with her mother's relatives. She sent me a letter and a picture of herself carrying a knapsack. She wrote that in the picture she was crossing the Arctic Circle and that it was the middle of the night and still light.

Elizabeth Mary finished the school year and went back to New York with Bobby.

Honorée didn't come back to school. In the late fall she sent me a letter and a picture of herself in cross-country ski clothes after the first snowfall.

I spent the summer in New York. Bobby, Elizabeth Mary, Antoinette, and I were a perfect circle of friends.

In the fall, when I was back in Iowa, Elizabeth Mary wrote me that she had a job offer for the following year, and that she and Bobby were thinking of getting married. Elizabeth Mary also discovered a job for me at a fairly good Catholic women's college near New York. We could all be together again.

That Christmas when I went back to New York I only saw Antoinette, Elizabeth Mary, and Bobby. Except of course for meeting the chairwoman who offered me the job on Elizabeth Mary's recommendation. Everything was getting simpler.

My remaining half year at Iowa was completely calm. My prospects kept me from being lonely. The only curious event was that Miss Quist called me in February. Her sorority had, in fact, sponsored her and she had been nominated for homecoming queen and had been voted runner-up, first princess in the queen's court. That had been in November. When she called me in February her voice sounded oddly different, much less pointed. She asked if she could come out to my house to talk about a problem. I said I was going to my office. She said she couldn't go there—would I stop by her room at her boarding-house? I hesitated and she said, "Please. I really need help."

When I got to the boardinghouse, she was waiting just inside the front door. I almost didn't recognize her. Her face was fat and puffy. She took my arm and gestured for me to come upstairs. Her landlady popped out of a door on the first floor and said, "Just one minute there, young lady." Miss Quist looked terrified. The landlady said, "This is approved housing and you're just not going to get away with this sneaking any-more of these men in your room." The landlady was spattering venom. I couldn't tell if I was an exhibit for the prosecution, the judge hearing her case, or the victim of Miss Quist's crime. The landlady went on, "I'd be within my rights to see your dean. You can't sneak away—there's those bad checks—"

"Just one," Miss Quist said.

"Oh ho! Well now, there's the one to me and then there's the drugstore—they called up here, you know. That's two, if you could ever bring yourself to tell the truth for once."

Miss Quist was beaten. The landlady saw it in her numb face. The landlady said, "What do you have to say to that? It's time you learned that most people pay for things. You came in here this fall all neat and pretty. Well, now look at you."

I finally said, "There's no need to be abusive." I loaned Miss Quist the money for her rent. We went out to the car and drove to the drugstore. I paid her debt while she waited in the car with her overcoat lapels pulled in front of her face. She wouldn't go anywhere where she might be seen. I took her back to my house for coffee. She kept her overcoat on. She was miserable, but her troubles with the world weren't as bad as she thought. Aside from the two checks, her first worry was that she'd gained twenty pounds. She'd been told by a psychologist at student health that the reason she'd done this was to make herself unattractive to men. I asked why the psychologist thought she wanted to do that. Miss Quist said that she'd stolen a dress from a store: she'd tried it on, gone back to the dress-ing room and simply put her own dress and coat on over it. Some days later a man who worked in the store stopped her in the street and accused her of stealing the dress. He said he might not have to tell anyone—he understood why a good-looker like her wanted a nice dress—but they'd have to talk it over since he might have to be responsible for the missing dress.

It struck me as an almost archaic mode. I pointed out that the clerk would be in an awkward position to press charges, now that he'd compromised himself.

Miss Quist said, "Oh, I know that. I even found out later he's married." She added grimly, "So he can't do a thing."

I asked what she thought this had to do with her gaining weight. She said, "I'm punishing myself and then I'm punishing men."

That sounded archaic too. I asked if she had any more problems.

She said, "Well, I just feel terrible. That's all it is now. I feel like crying all the time. I don't know anybody who's nice. So I thought if I could just talk to you, because the last time we talked you were so nice to me."

I was taken aback. I wondered if her memory was defective.

Miss Quist said, "You were really neat. I could change a lot if you just told me to."

I couldn't say anything for a moment.

"I know it sounds funny. But I can't go out with anyone and I can't go out anywhere. If I could just come out here and talk to you. You know, someone who isn't . . ." She sighed with exasperation.

"What about your psychologist?"

"Well, she's O.K. but she's tough. Look—we don't have to talk about me. I could read anything you said to and we could talk about that so it wouldn't waste your time. It's a new term now and I could sign up for independent study with you."

I said no to the independent study project, but I agreed to invite her out. We arranged that she come out Wednesdays at five for two or three weeks.

She took out a notebook and pen. "Look," she said, "I'll

write down a book I should read and I'll have to write down if I do it. Please."

I agreed.

It wasn't until her third visit that I understood what she *really* wanted. She wasn't being sly—she also wanted what she said she did. Since she wasn't going to class, I asked her to do her reading for her courses. She seemed smarter than I remembered. She was also diligent. She lost her puffy look. She showed me her chart in which she wrote down the miles she walked each day, the exercises she did, and even how many strokes she brushed her hair. She said that making herself report made her keep to her plan.

But what she most deeply wanted was magic.

She asked me if I heard from Honorée. I said I did.

"She really changed, didn't she?" Miss Quist said.

I said I wasn't sure.

"Oh, come on now. She really did." Miss Quist thought a moment. "Tell me what it was. Was it just things you told her? I know it was something different—I mean, I know she wasn't, you know, a girl friend. She didn't really seem to need boy-friends. I couldn't get over it. She jumped right over that whole business. She just skipped it, didn't she?"

I asked Miss Quist what she meant by the "whole business" of boyfriends. This wasn't a Socratic device. I wanted to know, and I had an odd sense of well-being talking to Miss Quist. I wasn't oppressed by any sense of her goodness or beauty, nor had she any interest in me—apart from my corporal works of mercy and what she hoped might be my magical, or sacramental, office.

She answered in a way that made me impersonally sympathetic. The whole business of boyfriends had been as oppressive to her as my life in boarding school to me. The people who had the power of real life and whose company she needed in order to enter real life were inferior to her in every way but one. They had the power of real life. They had it corporately rather than individually; she always felt at a loss toward the body at large. This swirl of fun, anxiety, and energy absorbed individuals and spewed them out. Most people she knew were unconscious of it.

I thought it was no wonder she'd wanted to be homecoming queen—or at least a princess in the court. She'd thought it was a formal incarnation of the "whole business" of boyfriends. Her disillusion must have felt awful. She had no sentimentality to cushion her feelings.

Now she thought that Honorée might have skipped over all that. She had to reexamine every word of her parody of Honorée's life. The whirlagig of time was certainly bringing in its revenges.

The next week Miss Quist asked me, just to be sure, if Honorée had been kicked out for being in a nude scene. I said no. Miss Quist asked if Honorée had got pregnant. I said no. Miss Quist asked me what Honorée was doing. I said that she was seeking adventure, change, and general knowledge of the kind that Honorée admired in Miss Chetty.

"Is she having fun?"

I said, "I think she is. I think she's happy."

Miss Quist said, "You know what she told me when we were still rooming together? I was teasing her about her crush on you and she admitted it—but she said that it didn't matter what you personally felt back because you were a connoisseur. I thought that was a real laugh—you know, Honorée trying out big words and not getting them right. I looked 'connoisseur' up in the dictionary the other day. What I want to know is what good it did her. What good could it have done her that"— Miss Quist looked at her pad—"that you were 'one competent to pass critical judgments in the arts, especially the fine arts'?"

I smiled at that. It struck me at first as being so typically Honorée. I said, "I don't think that's it. I really don't think there's any secret we can uncover. Honorée is just terribly nice." I was then alarmed by something in Honorée's remark. I said, "It's odd—I thought she liked me better than that. I mean, it sounds as though she may have meant something not entirely complimentary."

Miss Quist said, "Oh, come on. She really liked you."

Miss Quist felt better for reassuring me.

Miss Quist felt much better in general. Miss Quist transferred to Drake University, because it offered a program in "commercial design." Miss Quist wished to draw pictures for advertisements. She showed me her portfolio. I was able to say she had a knack.

I got a letter from Honorée. She was in Spain. She was traveling with a Swedish family, taking care of their children and teaching the children English. She thought that was amusing. She loved Spain in the spring, she loved the children. She didn't know what she would do for the summer.

I moved to New York at the beginning of the summer. Elizabeth Mary and Bobby were married two weeks after I got back. The reception was in Antoinette's apartment. Bobby had already rented another apartment two blocks farther south.

The ceremony was performed in a judge's chambers— Antoinette, Mr. Morse, and I were the only others there. There hadn't been a dinner the night before, so the guests with literary ambitions gave their toasts at the reception. This was an improvement: since the audience was on its feet and free to move about, the narrative impulse was diminished.

I was touched by Antoinette. She was very attentive to her father, who was clearly grateful. She gave a short toast, gallantly joking and punning. She produced some word play about her parents' intercontinental marriage and her father's cable address, and then referred to Bobby and Elizabeth Mary as "Am-Asian grace."

Antoinette was the center of this interior tableau. Clothes

had just begun to become bright again. Neckties were once again extravagant, and this was the first season of very short skirts. It struck me that fashion had taken on an air of costume, even of burlesque, an air which produced an effect of silly intimacy. How could one feel anything but playful around this maypole?

Bobby and Elizabeth Mary left. Antoinette saw her father leave—sober and in the hands of old friends. The other guests swirled for some moments and then began to drain out. The couple who'd catered began to pack up their glasses and trays.

Antoinette looked at me and laughed. She said, "You don't have to go, do you, Ollie? Ollie, Ollie in free."

The caterers wheeled out their two carts. I asked Antoinette if she'd like to go out to eat. She said yes, but then sagged into an armchair. She said, "Why don't you just fix us some eggs? Those ones you poach and then roll around a frying pan with all those herbs—you and Bobby used to do them."

When I came in from the kitchen I saw that she'd been crying.

I said, "I liked your toast. It reminded me of those postcards you used to send Bobby. Or the way you talked to him before you did those pairs competitions. Do you still skate?"

"Just for fun once in a while. God, I used to worry about Bobby. There wasn't any need. He was always calmer than I was. But when I was eighteen I didn't think either of you knew *anything*. I thought Bobby would be destroyed."

I said, "I still have the letter you wrote me—the one telling me not to worry about Josie. At first I was annoyed that Bobby told you about her and me. But then I loved it, it seemed such a French mode—advice to a raw youth from a clever beauty."

"What did I say?"

"It was about how to distract one's self from a broken heart. It was very funny. You signed yourself 'Your Aunt Juanette.' Would you like to see it? I could find it."

"Don't you dare."

"Well, it was wonderful—even just to learn you had painful crushes. The stories you'd told Bobby and me had terrified me—you were so masterfully funny about the boys you went out with. I was sure I'd be even more ridiculous to the girls I knew. But of course it was nice to hear the official school heroes mocked."

Antoinette sighed. "You make me think I was an awful bitch."

I thought she only half meant that. I said, "No. You were very witty, but you weren't ever seriously mean."

"That's because I wasn't ever serious."

"Oh, come on. You made Bobby's life possible. And you kept your father from feeling guilty—you gave him the feeling that being nice was all that was expected of him. Even when I was sixteen I could tell that. Bobby was my best friend—and your father was one of the few grownups I ever talked with naturally. So I could see your effect on them."

"And so I burned myself out from eighteen to twenty-two, building up two sweet, weak men."

I was amazed—I'd never imagined Antoinette as self-pitying.

I said, "Actually, you're more interesting now."

"Oh, Popeye," she said, "you're so stro-ong."

I thought that was mean. When I was a sixth former I monitored a study hall (all the prefects had something else to do that period). The lower formers used to call me Olive Oyl —derived from Oliver. Whenever I turned my back, one of them would laugh Popeye's laugh and another, implicitly taking my part, would chant in falsetto, "Ohh, Popeye! You're so stro-ong."

I said, "That, Auntie Juanita, is a painful memory."

But she didn't know what I was talking about. I explained. She said, "Oh—I only meant— Never mind. You know what I mean. One of those helpless things: 'What's a poor girl to do?' 'Ma, he's making eyes at me.' 'I'll bet you say that to all the

girls.' " Antoinette paused. "It's odd—you remember everything, don't you? For you, life is but an allusion." She slapped
her knee in a little parody of yukking it up. "But go on—tell
me more about how I'm more interesting now."

I said, "No. Let's go to the movies instead."

"Oliver! Are you asking me for a date? 'Be still, my
heart!' "

But through all her joking around I felt her wish for company. We saw a movie, took a walk, watched television, played
Ping-Pong. I spent the night in Bobby's old room.

While Bobby and Elizabeth Mary were away, Antoinette and I
conducted a courtship—or rather a self-conscious parody of
one.

At first the most serious question for her didn't seem to be
that of physical desire, but whether I could learn to converse in
her style. It was like learning to play Ping-Pong, which, cor-
relatively, I did.

But soon the effect of our conversation became more
powerful. About our present thoughts and feelings, our talk
was always indirect and joking. However, Antoinette loved
learning about my past thoughts and feelings in straightforward
detail. This thirst of hers for listening made my own history
seem suddenly lighter. My experiences seemed to dislodge
themselves in the telling; they seemed to float up and arrange
themselves for our amusement. The lighting was set too bright
for comedy. I felt relieved. The invisible ghosts of past embar-
rassments which used to brush my feelings unexpectedly were
condensed into bright fluttering visible figures, as harmless and
ornamental as butterflies.

This mood even had a reflection in my work. I no longer
pondered everything. I was no longer learning, slow with
worry. I could now rely on reflexes I'd been coiling up for
years.

I was worried that when Bobby and Elizabeth Mary came back, they might cast a dimming shadow. But they barely noticed Antoinette and me. They were seriously happy in their own style. So we were all elated at our new connections—connections which for Antoinette and me disconnected us from dismal earnestness. All summer long I was amazed at her ingenuity, at our ingenuity.

In the fall, I liked the disconnectedness of my job—I rode a commuter train against the flow of traffic. Out of the city in the morning and into the city in the afternoon. The students were well-schooled *jeunes filles bien élevées.* Many of them knew Latin and French and had read a good deal. If they were losing their faith, they lost it discreetly. The flavor of emotion in the best students was subtle. Their secrets, I suspected, bloomed like mushrooms. In any case, these secrets were not as crucial to me as those other secrets had been in Iowa.

Antoinette and I saw Elizabeth Mary and Bobby once a week. Bobby was happy that Antoinette was having a good time. He could tell she was more relaxed because she allowed him to show an old movie of them skating. Until recently she'd balked at looking at pictures of herself taken before the accident. I was stirred by Antoinette at twenty—she and Bobby skating away from the camera, their tight perky rumps tilted up like sparrows'. Antoinette looked fragile, except for her surprisingly full skater's thighs cased in brown, almost chocolate, nylons, much darker than her pale face.

Elizabeth Mary and I were all praise. Antoinette laughed, but allowed Bobby to show another reel. In the next short sequence I noticed what it was about Antoinette's face that had changed. It was really only her jaw that had been slightly curved to one side; it was not true that her face had been significantly more beautiful. She had been very pretty according to the style of the time—a style in which flawless delicacy came first. It was a face whose picture in a yearbook could start schoolboy daydreams of gazing and shy kissing. But what had been most appealing then was what was appealing now—the shy antagonism that kept her separate, that reserved to herself the last critical word on her performance. I understood why the physical accident, which now appeared physically less important, had undone her so.

Bobby had a whole carton of short reels, but he said that several of them needed to be repaired in some way. It turned out that the film laboratory he dealt with was not far south of Grand Central, so he asked me if I would drop them off and pick them up.

The next Monday, while I was waiting at the counter of the film processing company, I saw a man who looked familiar. He came up to me and I recognized him. He was Honorée's film director.

He said, "I know you. I'm sorry . . . I can't remember."

"Iowa," I said.

"Right. You're Honorée's teacher."

I was willing to let it go at that, but he seemed to want more. We talked. It turned out he was doing a documentary film about the *Catholic Worker*. It took me several questions to realize that he'd become unlapsed—or reconverted. The reason he wanted to talk was that he was ashamed about his time in Iowa, but in a curiously unembarrassed way. His memory, he admitted, was somewhat sketchy. He did know he'd been selfish. He now had a social conscience. In fact, he said, his social conscience had been awakened first. Then he ran into some people from the *Catholic Worker* and he realized that the *Catholic Worker* had been in there all along. And then he realized that the *Catholic Worker* people were only good because they loved Christ and it was Christ who had been in there all along.

His statement was not nearly as embarrassing as it sounds.

I asked him if he ever heard from Honorée. He said he hadn't. I asked him what had happened to "Hail Holy Queen."

That did embarrass him. He said he'd shown it in Iowa, and he'd been very ashamed of himself. He hadn't looked at it since —his whole life had changed.

I said that I would love to see it if it wouldn't trouble him.

He looked at me and said, "I remember now. You were there for the balloon part. I remember that."

"It was less than two years ago."

"I know," he said, "but one of those years was a long one. Look—you can see it. I'm pretty sure I have a print I can let you have."

He called me several days later and said he'd found the print. When I picked it up he warned me that the first half had gone gummy in spots. I wanted to pay him something. He refused, but finally accepted a contribution to his *Catholic Worker* film project.

As I left he said, "You ever hear from Honorée?"

"Yes, I just got a letter."

"If you write back say hi. Tell her I'll pray for her. I'm glad I ran into you, you know. This is O.K. about the film. It feels good."

I was struck by his sweetness because it was oddly impersonal. It was quite real—I had no doubt of that—but it was pleasantly disinterested.

I got Bobby to show me the film. We had to strip off part of the first half, but we finally got it going.

I was prepared for cute tricks. After all, Phil had said he was ashamed of it now. But it was wonderful. What was wonderful about it was that all the cute tricks, the studio effects, were funny in a less strained way—simultaneously rowdy, smart, and relaxed. Piety was mocked. That, of course, was expected. In fact, a lot of the early scenes were parodies of famous paintings or sculptural tableaux—*Adoration of the Magi, The Last Supper,* the *Pietà.* Phil had a good touch with making the actors flow into these set configurations—sometimes they would do a sort of double take as they fell into the picture; other times they went through the formal pose so fast that it was like a throwaway tag line.

But all this artificial comedy was distinctly framed by a sense of the natural world. While the mock pieties were on screen, the sound track blared appropriate confections—the Sanctus from the Berlioz *Requiem* or snatches of other sweet choral glory. But when there was an exterior—a field of black earth glazed with rain and giving off mists that steamed up to low clouds sliding by—there was silence. These moving pictures of landscape soon began to convey to me a sense of the natural world as an endless comfort (a feeling I never had when I had been *in situ*). No pathetic fallacy here: nature didn't sympathize; it was simply endless and other, but other in an attainable way, other but not alien, a stillness that will finally absorb all extravagance. It was as though Phil played out his quick-wittedness and delight in farce and mockery, and then laid them out as offerings to whatever was more formal and mysterious.

Of course, I'm in no position to make a perfect judgment. I brought a great deal of personal knowledge in the first place, and I've seen the film so many times that it is in danger of becoming a talisman. I have my own little projector now, which I keep in my study here (Bobby's old room). I've had the first part of the film cleaned, and the broken part respliced. If I look at the film only once every week or so, it is as fresh as ever. It is only when I let this habit get out of hand and run it more frequently—slowing it, stopping it, reversing it and advancing it, tantalizing myself by skipping over all the parts with Honorée in it or, worse, wallowing in those parts—only then, by intruding my control of time into the film's integral time, do I cause its enchantment to go a little dry. A two-week fast is then required to restore the enchantment. However, at the very

first screening my objective knowledge of these matters was intact and operable.

In the comic scenes of the pursuit of Honorée by the apostles, Honorée gaily flirts and flutters about until they have her
almost cornered. Then she disappears—poof!—and reappears
in the branches of a tree or on a rooftop. She looks surprised
and a little disappointed. As she clambers down and wanders
off, she is even somewhat awkward without the dance of the
chase. But later in the film she seems to become more graceful
on her own.

Phil had made fun of Honorée, but he had also admired
her. More than admired her. He'd used her to her advantage as
well as his. By the end his attitude toward her body is almost
the same as his sensual attitude toward the landscape, so that
her nakedness in the final sequence is not at all comic, as it had
been in the two or three earlier routines of tear-away robes and
gaping apostolic admiration.

Mary Magdalene's (that is, Honorée's) ascension is cleverly cut. It appears at first that she has suddenly sprouted wings
and risen. She examines her wings, radiates delight to be aloft.
I'd thought at the time of the filming that her face had been
blank, but the zoom-lens close-ups are clear. But then—deliberately, I think—the devices are exposed. The camera pulls
back to show the harness, the shrouds, and then the balloon.
Then the cameraman on the roof. Then his clumsy attempt to
catch the balloon. Then some hasty shots of the balloon in its
cross-lots flight, until it finally disappears over the oak trees
near the river.

Phil must have gone back later to shoot more film of the
same part of the landscape. The portions of landscape become
longer and longer in between shots of the balloon. The final
minute of film is nothing but countryside.

He got it just right: The chalkiness of the pressed gravel
and white dust on the roads. The bosomy low roundness of the
rising ground. The stillness of the shadows in the stands of

trees. The glimmer of streams flowing in easy curves through the square fields. Of course, the fields are square only in conception; they heave up and bend with the motion of the land. The fence lines and straight furrows are really arcs pinned at either end in dells or stream beds.

The very last shot is of a road—a straight, unstoppable bright ribbon rising and falling and reappearing crest after crest. I've since realized that three arcs of road can suggest endlessness. There is no greater suggestion of openness or promise, unless it's the flat undersides of the clouds seeming to extend the design beyond the horizon, promising more space in which it is certain that the road continues to rise and fall.

Bobby recognized Honorée. He'd even noticed my Volkswagen in one of the hectic shots toward the end. I'd missed it. He mentioned all this casually. He'd enjoyed the film, but he didn't intrude on what must have appeared to him as my intense interest.

I got him to show me how to operate the projector.

Not long after that, but before I'd decided I'd better show the film to Antoinette, I got another letter from Honorée. She'd come back to America with some other Americans she'd run into in Scotland. She didn't say what she'd been doing in Scotland. She was currently living in a commune in Arizona, helping to build buildings she described as "breakthroughs." They were some sort of dome made of old car bodies. She enclosed a photograph of herself wearing a tilted-back welder's mask and holding an acetylene torch.

She wrote: "We use the excesses of society. It is possible to live off the land and do no harm. That is what many people don't understand. Although we have the support of many other people. I wish you could come here. You'd scarcely recognize me I bet. I tried to adopt an Indian baby which a lawyer I met said was possible for unmarried people and that he would help, but the agency refused and he never came back as he said he would. If you come, bring warm clothes and a sleeping bag as it is cold at night although hot during the day. You are in my thoughts and prayers. Love, Honorée."

It sounded as though she didn't have much time to write out there. She was back to "Our dog is named Kartoffel." I liked the motherly touch at the end about warm clothes. Also "thoughts and prayers." Her Lutheran mother undoubtedly had just written that to her. Probably surreptitiously—Honorée had mentioned in an earlier letter that her father had disowned her. But faithful old mutti sent her thoughts and prayers. And so to me.

I left the letter and snapshot out for Antoinette to see.

After she'd discovered them and taken them in, she held up the picture at me. "Hmm—this is the Miss Hogentogler you told me about. In her new role as Rosie the Riveter." But she immediately softened. She said, "She's sweet. It's odd—so many people are sweeter these days. At least . . . I don't know why. Or maybe I don't know why *we* were so cross. Except Bobby—Bobby was sweet all along."

I knew what she meant. It was easy at that point to invite her to watch the film.

Elizabeth Mary and Bobby came over for supper, and afterward I put the film on.

"Ah ha," Elizabeth Mary said when the credits came on. "Phillip McMahon was a student of mine." She didn't notice Honorée's name, but recognized her when she appeared.

When the film ended after the shot of road looping away over low hills, Elizabeth Mary said, "It's like the end of *A Nous la Liberté*. René Clair."

I didn't mind this secondary opinion.

As my past had become lighter in my improved present, now the present became lighter in the face of the film. It wasn't that I forgot the improvement in my life, but while I contemplated the film, the present was pulled away like foreground mist blown off to reveal a vanishing point in the distance.

I ran the film backward and then forward again through

the final sequence. I can't go to Arizona, I thought. I would burn in the sun. I wouldn't like those people. I am devoted to Honorée in other ways. I ran the film backward and then forward again. Here is how I secretly worship, by these clouds and arcs of road, although this is just the image of them.

TESTIMONY

AND

DEMEANOR

I SHOULD NEVER HAVE COME TO NEW
York. I do the work O.K. I guess. But everything else is
hard. I talk to myself. At least in law school I had room-
mates. I didn't like them, but we could always talk. About how
we didn't like law school. Here I come back to this apartment—
and I admit the apartment is my fault, I don't have very good
taste—anyway, I come back to the apartment at 10 p.m. and
talk to myself. Approximately the same conversation every
night.

"Work hard today, Charlie?"

"Nothing special. Usual fifteen hours."

"If you were as slick as some, you could have done it in
twelve. I suppose you'd like a drink."

"Don't mind if I do."

"I suppose you still drink rye."

"I suppose I'm still a hick."

"Why don't you go back to New Hampshire? Do a little
work for the electric company. Get backed for the state legisla-
ture. Go home where people notice your hard work. I suppose
you're going to work this Sunday?"

"Only a half day."

"Why not the whole day? You got anything better to do?"

One drink and in my state of mind I'm plowed. I speed-
read a detective novel and fall asleep by midnight. Every night.

No, I don't even admire my endurance anymore. And
there's not much besides that.

Yes, I work late even when I don't have that much to do. I just
let it stretch out. Today I know I could have left before supper.
I also realized I know the new I.R.S. regs by heart. But there's
no way anyone could find out. Mr. Leland remains a guarded
mystery behind his secretary. And I stay in my broom closet. I

even know the sections on farm income. I read them for no reason at all.

One of the partners I worked for last year came down to ask me out for lunch.

"Young man, it's time for lunch. Get your hat."

I got up, smiled, said I didn't wear a hat.

He said, "Let me know when you get one and we'll arrange lunch."

Honest to God.

Maybe I could find my freshman beanie.

That was so weird that I barely noticed it, but later in the day I went uptown to deliver some things by hand—I didn't have to but I wanted out. Just for an hour or so. On the street I ran into a girl I'd known when she was at Bennington. She was going to an art gallery. I needed some more time out, so I went along. She cross-examined me on my job. I said I was helping fat cats to stay fat. She said that was awful. At length. I'd been through everything she said, but I was pleasant enough. I listened, agreed, and even sharpened up some of her arguments.

But she wanted to know how I felt *personally.* "Personally," I said, "if it's still the same after five years, I'll go back to the woods."

"Five years," she said.

"Counting from when I started," I explained.

Five years was beyond her. We stopped talking about it. But I had listened to her on the subject. And when we ran into some guy she knew at the art gallery, and he walked around with us, saying this and that about the pictures, I listened to him too. I finally spoke up myself about one I liked, saying it looked like Portsmouth in a fog. The two of them exchanged glances. I hadn't said I thought it *was* Portsmouth in a fog; obviously it was some place in Portugal since the painter's name was da Silva. They began to make remarks after that—"I think this one is a geodetic survey." "No. A Coca-Cola bottling plant in Secaucus." I said I had to get back to work, but the other fellow left first.

"Don't mind him," she said, as though it had been all him. "He takes this all very seriously. Pure art, and you have a very literary taste."

"You mean *literal*," I said.

"No," she said. She brushed something off my shoulder. She didn't explain. She asked after some college friends of mine she'd known, and then she left.

I minded. Why is it that dumb people with "taste" get away with it and smart people without taste don't? I am patient and I run my own life. What the hell.

Yesterday I felt how boxed in I am. Or maybe boxed out. Today another partner, Mr. Charles Pelham, popped in. I have nothing to do with him as far as work goes. He just dropped in and started talking. There was a while when some of the associates used to wander by and look in as though the corridor was a zoo. I could get rid of them. Mr. Pelham can get away with it, I suppose. But I don't have to like it. A regular cross-examination.

He asked me—inter alia—if I was religious. I said no.

He said, "That's what Franklin Roosevelt said. Said he preferred not to think about those things. Odd, don't you think?"

Odd is right. He asked me if I was a humanitarian, aesthete, epicurean, adventurer. A few others I can't remember. Then he asked me if I'd ever wanted to be a woman.

I said, "Are you asking me if I'm homosexual?"

"No," he said. "That would be a different question. That question would be 'Are you a homosexual?' This question is 'Have you ever wanted to be a woman?' But perhaps I should ask first, 'Have you ever considered at length what it would be like to be a woman?' "

Nope.

"And yet you have imagination."

I said, "I don't know." I was getting sore. "I'm probably a robot."

He brightened up. "Would you like to be a robot?"

When I didn't answer, he said, "If you can save various of our clients millions in taxes you surely have imagination. I'm not one to despise our work here. In fact, I think the tax structure of this country ranks with the pyramids. If you simply consider the labor . . . Later generations will surely wonder at us, as we wonder how on earth the Egyptians ever got those stones to the top. And taxes are as metaphysical as any theology. Angels on pins aren't a patch on us. And we're so various. A warp and woof of contending nominalism and realism. If one only had the swiftness of mind to see it all at once, to compass it, I imagine it would be as intricately alluring as a Persian carpet. I've often thought that only Proust and our tax structure stand up to a good Persian carpet. Don't you think? I mean, in one sense the tax structure is art—a subsuming of the infinite muddle of human activity under a single rubric, as though it had a single purpose and could be ordered by a mind hewing to the line of a single vision. Everything that everyone is doing this very instant in this part of town has tax consequences. Do you ever feel the impact of that? But I imagine you have your own comparisons. I once was possessed by the thought that our tax officials were like Satan in the Book of Job. Congress is like God. And the taxpayer is Job. 'Then Satan answered the Lord, Doth Job fear God for nought? Hast not thou made a hedge about him and about his house and about all that he hath on every side?' and so forth. '. . . and his substance is increased in the land. But put forth thine hand now, and touch all that he hath, and he will curse thee to thy face.' You see? 'And the Lord said unto Satan, Behold, all that he hath is in thy power'? And that is the tax system. But I imagine you have your own comparisons."

I began to look down at my desk and up at him and down at my desk again. He mumbled something and popped out. I should have said taxation reminded me of a Coca-Cola bottling plant in Secaucus.

But as I think of it, I get the impression that although he was talking ninety-nine percent of the time, he was trying me out, fishing for me. The trouble is he was using too fancy a lure. If he'd just asked me how I did in law school. Or how I liked New York. Good old worms like that. But he's too good a talker to bother with anything easy. Like Cardozo writing an opinion. You don't know what it means but you remember it. ". . . not merely honor but a punctilio of an honor the most sensitive." I'll never forget it, but I'll never use it, and neither will anybody else.

Being able to work in a concentrated way is a great advantage. I shouldn't have complained. I knocked off everything projected for the next three days in one single day. I got into it for three hard hours, and just when I felt myself slowing up I bore down for another three, ate a sandwich, and put in another three just coasting downhill toward supper. Ate, walked around the block, and rounded out the day with a last three which could have been two but I didn't want to get careless. I won't have to touch a thing I did today. I may have to take a half hour to explain the memo to Mr. Leland so he can explain it to the client, but it's all there. All there in one neat package. I was worried that I'd been slowed up. No one else in the world could have done that piece of work in one day.

Mr. Pelham dropped by again. I'd just got back from presenting the memo to Mr. Leland. Mr. Leland was impressed, so I wasn't bothered by the prospect of Mr. Pelham being cute again with his cultural quiz. But he started off in low. For him, that is. He actually asked me how I'd got along in law school. And he waited for an answer.

I told him that what gave me whatever edge I'd had—since I was clearly no Frankfurter—was a capacity for work and for organizing other people's ideas. Right away I saw there were some minds which were quick and subtle. Some of them could grind too, and they went on to be *Law Review*. But some of them had no organizing power. They were happy to break up a problem in class. Suggest all the difficulties. Sometimes I wasn't even sure I understood all of them. But having done all that work out loud—scored a few points for wit and elocution—they'd be tired of it. Maybe bored. That was *their* problem. I picked up the pieces. Not all the little cute ones. Early on I figured out that if you put too fine a point on an argument it's likely to arouse suspicion. Ingenious but unsound, as the saying goes. Which means baloney is baloney no matter how thin you slice it.

The other thing I found out was not to waste time with my gut reactions. It was amazing to see how many bright guys kept on getting wrapped up in long-winded arguments, as though this or that case was the last chance to reform the country. Ninety-nine out of a hundred cases, even in textbooks, are narrow questions. You don't have to start with the Bill of Rights every time.

There was another way that guys who might have started out smarter than me went wrong. They wouldn't finish the question. They would find all the issues and go on and on about the rights and wrongs, but they'd forget that at the end you've got to be exact about who gets what. People don't go into court to improve their minds.

But the main advantage came from not resisting the process. There were a few who could still be the fair-haired boys of the faculty in their defiance of the assumptions necessary to the workings of the law—in fact, a little fair-haired defiance is itself necessary to the workings of the law school. But many more people foundered because they were afraid they might be brainwashed away from some mental set they'd grown fond of—sometimes it was some political ideal, but more often it was some notion of themselves as too complex and humane to fit into the mold of just being a lawyer. A mere lawyer. To me there was nothing mere about it.

When I got through with this explanation—and it's not a bad outline of how to overachieve with a B mind—Mr. Pelham said he couldn't wait to hear more tomorrow but now he had to go. He left. But there isn't any more.

Now comes Mr. Pelham to—to what?

Mr. Pelham: "Deferred expectations bother me more than anything. Going to law school, if one is serious, is tedious. One banks on the future. And three years pass. But the hopes that practice will be zestfully different are soon dashed. One's manhood is not fulfilled. The new deferment is for five years. In five years the increment of skill, authority, and seniority will have made one's life one's own again. And I suppose thirty or thirty-one is not too late to start in. And yet it seems to me that people not only acquire the habit of work, which is not so bad—I rather like work, about half of the time—but they also have acquired the habit of deferring their expectations. Perhaps indefinitely. Occasionally one sees our young partners acquiring an energy for some project. They go to Washington or to an international conference. They are radiant and eager, but they are on a short tether. They return. There are others who never leave. I think they spend their real feelings in the bosom of their family in some umbrageous suburb. But either way everything is moderate. Moderated. That great leap forward will not be. But then, I suppose this is true in general. Immigrants used to defer their expectations to their children. Orwell once said that working-class Englishmen were middle-aged in their thirties because they gave up living for themselves, surrendering unconditionally to their jobs and families. In fact, he said they even *look* old. You can always find someone worse off.

"But adventure . . . Don't you have the feeling that there was a class of people—perhaps in the eighteenth century, perhaps in the seventeenth—who could imagine no other way to live but toward an adventure that would illuminate their lives? When did they succumb? When did we succumb? I sometimes suspect adventure declined because of nineteenth-century genius. Nowadays no one dares to build a monument to his own passion—be it family, nation, creed, romantic love—because one knows that before long someone with a Ph.D. in Darwin, Freud, or Marx will come along and dissect it as an example of something doomed, repressed, unnatural. I have nothing against dissection or even vivisection. No brief against the academics at all, but rather against those who are intimidated. They are frightened of shadows. What they need is more disbelief. If one is frightened of being a pejorative example, one only has to believe his own sayings instead. I yearn to hear someone say, 'My life is superb by no standard but my own adoration of it. I am not improving the world, I am not the wave of the future, I am not aiding any scheme of history or nature.' "

Mr. Pelham stopped abruptly. "That sounds terrible, doesn't it? Reminds me of what's-his-name. 'Black as the night that covers me. Di-da-da-dum from pole to pole. I thank whatever gods may be for my unconquerable soul.' Terrible. Roosevelt liked it—publicly at least. But I was doing well until then. Up to 'by no standard but my own adoration of it.' "

I checked around and found that Mr. Pelham doesn't do this to anyone else—not recently anyway.

My days have been peaceful for two weeks. Mr. Pelham has been in Japan (a Japanese conglomerate is one of our clients). I found I missed his visits. But today he got back and gave me a good half hour on the Japanese. Boring? I'm telling you. A few headnotes: Japanese forms of prayer. Japanese childhood.

Japanese food. Japanese attitudes toward career. Failure of psychiatry in Japan. About five minutes per item. But he kept it moving along. He said he thought I would like the Japanese.

Maybe he wants me to work for him when I get through with Mr. Leland. Not on my program if I can help it.

Today—a week after Japan—he gave me a lecture on paternity. His attitude toward it. Sort of a moot point since he isn't married and is over sixty, I'd guess.

Mr. Pelham: "I would have liked to have a son who was extremely gifted in, let us say, music or painting but whose attitude toward his work was so intense that he refused to discuss it. And perhaps he would be somewhat inarticulate anyway. By way of reaction to his father. However, having known him for, let us say, twenty-four years, I would be in a unique position to perceive his state of mind as it emerged in his work. I would know almost all the variables. Imagine the possibilities of appreciation in that situation."

Mr. Pelham paused, as usual, just before winding up, and, as usual, wound up with a crack at himself. "Yes, I would have been a great stage mama lurking in the wings."

Apparently when he's doing business he doesn't talk this much.

Today for the first time he showed up twice. The second time was just for a minute as I was leaving for supper. He caught me in the hall and asked me what I read. I told him detective novels. He seemed to be waiting for more, so I told him (which was true when I was at law school and couldn't get to sleep) histories of military campaigns.

"*Seven Pillars of Wisdom?*" he said. "Francis Parkman?"

"World War Two," I said. "I don't know why."

"How interesting," he said in that you've-flunked-your-cultural-quiz way. If he thinks I've flunked, why doesn't he go talk to one of the three-piece suits custom made in London?

He brought me a book today that he said was a Japanese general's account of the taking of the Philippines. Now I'll have to read it.

I asked him why he thought I'd like the Japanese.

A: "Because technical progress didn't disrupt their inner life, although now they couldn't live without it."

Query that.

I whipped through the book last night and it wasn't bad. Well detailed. The author wasn't afraid of details. A lot of American accounts are boring precisely because all they want to talk about is hitting the beaches so they can sell to the movies. This Japanese general went into decision-making when you only know a fraction of the variables and you're not sure *what* fraction. There were unfortunately a lot of fragments of poems, which might have helped if I knew the whole thing, as I suppose the reader is supposed to. "The clouds linger by mountain peaks." That sort of clue. Thanks a lot.

But what is interesting is this: I went upstairs to leave the book off. Mr. Pelham was across the hall in a conference room. As I left his office, the conference room door opened and there he was with some Japanese, speaking Japanese. Just gargling away. He talked to me twice about Japan and never said he spoke the language. I'm not saying that if you speak a foreign language you tell everyone you meet, but he had a whole week of chances and he is not a man to hide what he knows.

Mr. Pelham: "What is interesting about you is that you have no group to report to. I had the handicap of knowing a number of interesting people in college and some time thereafter (alas, not all of them interesting anymore), and therefore almost every pleasurable experience I had I spoiled somewhat by thinking how I was going to report it. Of course, the reporting itself was something of a pleasure. And I suppose even 'the seeking out of pleasurable experiences in order to report them was a pleasure, so perhaps I didn't lose—although it wasn't until I was past forty that I discovered pleasures that were isolated, unlinked to any imaginary audience of friends or friend. I sometimes think we've reached a stage of such social density that almost all pleasures are vicarious. Certainly echoic, in that they are transmutations of a small band of original visions generally unknowable. Brahms conceives in pleasure (let us assume, although perhaps he didn't). He scribbles down what he heard. The performer gets it second-hand, and we get it third-hand from him. Now, one theory is that the original Platonic shimmering whole that Brahms glimpsed through the clouds becomes less perfect with every communication of it. But another theory, perhaps my own, is that the original vision actually has very little to recommend it except Brahms' rendering of it. And it is only enhanced, not lessened, in its successive stages. Not inevitably but possibly; good vicars are necessary. Good translators. If we can assume them, then nothing is lost in translation—on the contrary. The primitive vision was not of paradise (there is none); it was only a quirk of one mind. Providing that the successive receivings and retransmittings are done by minds as rich—and why not?—the original is augmented. In fact, the pleasures of Proust's life were nothing to write home about. But I like Proust's liking them. And I like even more my liking of Proust's liking. I've gotten as much pleasure *remembering* my reading Proust as I ever did reading Proust.

"But then, perhaps the most complete pleasure of all would be to know the original germ, be aware of its injection into a mind, see its growth *ab ovo*, and follow its passage from mind to mind, sensing the entire cycle of enrichment. Until at last one saw—one witnessed—the whole ornate growth entering one's own mind." Mr. Pelham paused. "And decaying there in a sterile vacuum. I refer to my lawyer-like habit of being an objective observer in the vortex of other people's passions."

He left on that note. But I thought it was his best day so far.

Mr. Pelham: "It was you I meant to speak of yesterday. I'm sorry. I was distracted by myself again. And yet it's sometimes instructive to follow a chance phrase. I noted that you have no group to report to. But what I really meant to say is that you seem immune to other people's psychic disturbances. Quite the opposite from me. I am almost too conscious. I would be particularly susceptible to *folie à deux*. Even when I'm talking to you I find myself revolving around your stolidity. You come from New Hampshire, don't you? The Granite State. Dartmouth too. What is that song? 'We have the granite of New Hampshire in our muscles and our minds.'"

I said that was an old joke.

"I'd like you to meet a group of people," he said after a minute. "Mostly much older, but often much sillier. Than you. I'm not sure. . . . Some of the women are very attractive. For some reason, especially on Sunday afternoons. Especially in the fall. There's something about the light. Tired yellow sunlight on the sides of empty buildings. I can't imagine why people leave New York to go to the country."

I said I'd come and he told me where he lives.

I've been here two years today. Still going strong. Mr. Leland noticed the anniversary and said he'd noticed the amount of work I was doing. My health is good. I maintain my level in the

Canadian Air Force exercise book. I drink less than I did in law school. Work doesn't get me down while I'm doing it. Only occasionally at night, after it's done.

What are my weaknesses? I think my ambition is less in a general way. I shy away from arguments that are general. And I must learn to maintain my point of view with something more than just answers.

I went to Mr. Pelham's Sunday afternoon. Only a half dozen people. That was worse than a crowd. All older. One very old woman named Eleanor and two middle-aged ones. All three of them are divorced.

Everyone was playing a word game. The game was what words can you do without (in connection with yourself) when you're over fifty? They all sat around suggesting words that had a tendency to be a little tough, a little too serious. I mean, they're none of them young.

A man said, "Hope." They hemmed and hawed over that. Someone said, "Innocence."

A woman with straw-colored hair said, "I'm not sure, but we can certainly do without the pretensions of innocence."

They all said, "Ahh."

"Infatuation."

"No," the woman with the straw-colored hair said. "*Au contraire.* It's a word you wouldn't *think* of using in connection with yourself *until* you're at least forty."

Someone said, "Pride."

The other middle-aged woman said, "But not vanity."

"Fertility."

Same lady, who had a deep tan and black hair with a white streak, said, "Thank God." But I think she was putting on being brassy, since she looked the youngest. Maybe forty-five.

There was a pause in the game. Mr. Pelham said, "Perhaps we should examine the seven deadly sins."

The tan lady said, "Is that all there are?" They all laughed and she looked pleased.

A fat man said, "I'm sure you'll find them all intact for years, my dear."

Mr. Pelham said, "Well, no. I found, for example, that when I reached the age of fifty I was no longer bothered by envy."

I found that interesting.

The fat man said, "What about the five senses?"

The lady with the straw-colored hair said, "I hope old age doesn't find any of us tasteless."

The fat man said, "Oh, very good."

The tan lady said, "Sensitivity," cutting in on the straw-haired lady's applause. "I mean being upset, you know, going around being *wounded.*"

"Righteousness," the fat man said loudly.

The lady with the straw-colored hair turned to me and said, "What do you think? Aren't you playing? That keen legal mind..."

"Acne," I said.

She said, "Oh, *quelle horreur.*"

The tan lady with the silver streak laughed and said to Mr. Pelham, "And you told me he didn't have a sense of humor."

Mr. Pelham laughed at her, although he could tell I'd heard what she'd said. Didn't seem to bother him.

The game went on for a while and then died. I went over to talk to the lady with the straw-colored hair. Mrs. Morr. She talked to me about ballet, for some reason. I couldn't think of anything to say so I finally asked her if she used to do it herself.

"Oh, when I was a very little girl," she said. She curled up in the corner of the sofa and looked like a little girl. I suppose I stared at her. It was sort of a shock, no, a surprise, since she'd looked pretty good from the start, but she looked suddenly very flirtatious and I realized that the whole thing—her outfit, her gestures, her looking off to one side to show off her nose—the whole thing right along had been meant to be attractive and I just hadn't noticed. I'd just been talking to her because she seemed the most talkative. Even by comparison with Mr. Pelham. Anyway, it suddenly took hold. What it was was this—I don't think of the girls I used to know as women, even the ones now married and with kids. Just as I don't think of anyone I know who's my age (including myself) as a man. There seems to be no marking the change from high school to college to law school to working for a firm. Just more intensity. The more they pour on, the more you learn to handle. But Mrs. Morr was beyond all that. She didn't have to do anything, and there was a pleasant sense of drift to her when she opened up. It was clearly just for the fun of it. Like a great big sunny flower.

After a minute she jangled her bracelets up to her elbow and held her empty glass up over the back of the sofa. Mr. Pelham glided in to pick it up.

"Very, very weak," she said. "I'm practically under sedation."

But I didn't care if she talked like that from time to time as long as she could be free and easy.

I asked her what all the people did for a living. The fat man was a professor of economics. Keller. Herr Doktor Keller, she called him. The lady with the silver streak had worked in advertising until she got a divorce and retired. ("That's a switch," I said, and realized I'd caught on a little slow. But Mrs. Morr laughed as though I'd made the joke.) The old lady had written some mystery stories. They all seemed to like her a lot. The other man besides Mr. Pelham and Mr. Keller owned a shipping line. Mrs. Morr hadn't ever asked him what kind of ships.

I asked her what she did.

She said, "Well, last week I reassured all my friends. Next week I'll get them to reassure me. The week after I don't know what I'll do. Perhaps you could suggest something."

"Don't look at me," I said, "I'm just an employee. Tote that barge. Lift that bale." I realized I was trying to sound like her and missing by a lot. I sounded like someone at a fraternity rush.

"I hear you work very hard," she said.

When she said that, which was such a set remark (although I was glad she didn't say nothing), I realized that a lot of the rest of her remarks she made up on the spot under a certain kind of pressure. It made me think of answering questions in class at law school. Except she didn't refer to a subject; she referred to herself. She let you know about her mood. More than that. She made her mood change and tried to get you to follow each change. She also made me wonder what she would say if I ever caught up with her and pinned her down about anything.

Probably nothing. Feelings are feelings, not ideas, and she'd just keep on blowing bubbles.

I had to wait till today (Tuesday) to see Mr. Pelham. He asked me if I'd had a good time. I said sure. He said, "I was intrigued. I wouldn't have thought Ann Morr was your dish of tea. Connie Wentz"—the tan lady with the silver streak—"now there is a robust charm. She had a remarkable tan, don't you think? Right after she was divorced, she bought a little yawl she keeps finding young men to sail for her while she suns herself. She loves being at sea. Very exuberant. Fogs, storms, sunny breezes. She was going to name her yawl the *Alimony*. It seemed to me needless provocation, and after our conversation she named it the *Applecart*."

Next Sunday. At Mrs. Morr's apartment. Mr. Pelham asked me. When I got there, Mrs. Morr answered the door. She seemed surprised to see me. I was embarrassed, which she noticed. I said something like I should have waited to come with Mr. Pelham so she'd be able to place me.

She said, "No, no, no. I certainly place you—certainly, after all your gallant attentions. It's just that you're an hour early."

I said I'd come back, then, and started to go. She took me by the arm and said, "No, don't be the least embarrassed. I'm flattered you're so on time." She led me into the living room, chattering away. "Come into my parlor, said the spider to the fly. Do sit down. I won't be a minute. Actually several—you know, the preparational mysteries, getting my teeth out of the glass. God, I'd better be careful. Lawyers believe everything you say against yourself, isn't that the rule? You don't believe that, do you? What I'm really doing— You *did* believe it, didn't you?"

I said, "No, I didn't. It was just that you were talking so fast."

She said, "I do do that."

I said, "You look very pretty." Suddenly. Jesus.

She said, "Oh, la, how flattering," as though it were perfectly all right. But I think she must have been embarrassed too. Fortunately she left.

When she got back it was a half hour later, so we only had a half hour to go. I'd been thinking of what to talk about. Either some more about ballet—that is, get her started again— or get her to say more about the people who were coming. That looked like a better bet (longer), but she didn't do much with it. I asked her if there was some reason for them all to get together, some interest they all had.

She said, "We're all old, old friends, and we don't expect very much, but for some reason each of us cares what happens to the others." She said it earnestly, for her, as though it were a summation of a more detailed statement.

I didn't get it all, but it ended that line. So for some reason I started talking about having worked for two years in New York and how I'd tried to figure out what was wrong—not that I thought there was anything wrong, but that I'd suddenly felt cut off from my original plans, which were still all I had to go by. I said, "I thought that I shouldn't get into problems that took away energy for no purpose. Energy always seemed to me the main problem. The question always was: how to keep it up. How to keep it efficient. So I kept away from anything static."

She said, "I imagine that's a very exciting way to be."

I realized that I didn't really have control of what I was talking about. But I said, "No. It's gone on so long it's not exciting. It—I mean trying to focus my energy—was the only way to begin. I know I'm not being specific." She nodded. "It's gone on for a long, long time now, because at first I thought it was the only way, and then I didn't dare let up. And now I don't dare stop any habit, because something might depend on it. But there *are* other ways. I've seen some of the other people at work. Some of them are duds, but some of them are up to the job, and they don't need the control that I exercise. In fact, they don't even seem to need energy. I'm not envious. I don't mind doing what I have to do competitively. That's not something I'd ever complain about. But I have the feeling that there is something else I could do. Something else I could know. I have the feeling sometimes that there are people who know me down to the ground and I don't know the first thing about them."

She said, "Oh, lawyers in a bunch are terrifying. I used to have lunch near Wall Street once a month, and just the sight of all those dark suits marching out to lunch in phalanx . . . I was sure they'd all march over to me and—oh, I don't know—cross-examine me." She began to stroke her throat. "I could never even picture Charles"—Mr. Pelham—"holding his own somehow, even though he's the smartest man I know. It seemed like such a militant concentration of grim energy." She smiled. "Of course, you were speaking of your own grim energy, I know, but I think I can imagine what it would be like to live with nothing but that. Really, you know, Dickens' blacking factory is nothing next to a modern career. I mean, I do understand you, don't I? All you know are lawyers who are grim or who at least act grim with you, and that includes yourself—I suppose that is your point, that you are the grimmest of them all."

I nodded.

We sat there awhile in silence, but she smiled off into the distance so I didn't feel that I had to say anything.

She said, "Well, there really is nothing . . . I mean, here I am, a wise old crone without a word of wisdom."

We sat some more. I pieced together that every time she refers to being old she is testing to see that no one takes her seriously. I also noticed that part of her attractiveness is her style—for example, I get the impression that her clothes are so much a part of her style that touching them would be like touching her. When the doorbell rang she let it ring three or four times without getting up, and when she did get up she looked back a couple of times. I got it—that is, the point she was making—but she can do these polite gestures better than anyone I've ever seen. Mr. Pelham arrived and then the whole gang, along with some others. I'm glad to see that they get in some fresh air.

Mr. Pelham has finally given up talking about Connie Wentz. He started right in on Ann. Almost like the first day of questions.

"Do you think Ann is intelligent?"

I said that although she doesn't solve any problems, she probably could if she'd been educated differently.

"But there is an intelligence in her charm?"

I said that she was able to suggest her feelings in a way that made other people share them, which meant that she must appreciate how other people felt in the first place. A form of intellection.

"But there is a great deal that is unexpected in her feelings. There are some quite bizarre tastes that one could never share but that are nevertheless vastly appealing to hear about."

I didn't know what he was talking about. But I said, "Some of your notions are pretty far-fetched too. From where I stand, you're both apt to say some pretty strange things."

"But you would distinguish between our sensibilities? Between our minds?"

I said, "Oh, you just proceed in the same way. There are substantive differences."

"Surely you remember the elementary lesson of *Erie* versus *Tompkins*," he said. "Procedure and substance are inextricably intertwined." He paused. "But isn't it amazing how little we can actually say on a subject of mutual interest? The barrier of our common legal training."

II

One of the things I have begun to think about is that although I get embarrassed I'm not shy.

Actually, what I thought about this afternoon was that anytime I could just get up and go over to see her. She is just there. Of course not. She is there the way the clouds linger around the mountain peaks or whatever it was.

I see the satisfaction that Mr. Pelham takes in thinking about himself. I thought today: I have discovered taste. Taste is a discernible pattern in voluntary noncareer decisions. I had bad (no) taste in women. I thought, while I was in college, that it was natural that girls were sullen. I could understand why they were sullen—I'm surprised I wasn't more sullen myself. Except I had more anesthesia. The arrangements were enough to sullen up anyone. To wit—arrive by train at White River Junction. Enough to account for sullenness right there. Barely recognize me from previous unpleasant (and dark) arrangement. Dull afternoon shadowed over for her by thought of basic decision, which was: Would she submit? "Submit" is the word. Unspoken struggle. If she had more than three drinks, the unspoken rule was, that meant yes. If she went to my room without stating a formal objection, that meant yes. On my side it was necessary to express minimal formulae of traditional courtship. And the final burst of energy to overcome our indifference, which was our largest bond of sympathy. That was when I discovered that although I was easily embarrassed I wasn't shy. Another way of stating the concept is: There was more social pressure preventing me from disengaging from the mechanism of the weekend than there was embarrassing personal pressure impeding its progress. I remember noting that there were cranks who rejected the process and who were miserable, and then, of course, there were a few who transcended it. I thought they might have transcended it by dint of repeating it over and over. In any case, they looked much happier on the railroad platform at White River Junction. They also drank a lot less.

But even so, I never spent any time questioning that the function of the weekend was to make the solitude of the week a comparatively attractive alternative. Energy was still the key concept. For the most part I withheld energy from the weekend (except for rationed bursts to avoid inertia). Otherwise there seemed no way or reason to spend it. To be without energy at that time (1957–61) was considered an average, prudent, and reasonable way to behave.

There is no point in regretting it—I wouldn't have come as far as I have if I hadn't lived that way. But now I welcome the chance to see Mrs. Morr act freely. To feel her extravagance. She is, as far as I know, without a goal, but she is capable of reaching one if she chooses. Therefore her actions are freer than anyone's I've known. And until she has a goal, also more extravagant. She has had a marriage. She is accomplished. She is detached. I suppose I should be careful not to absorb any of her extravagance.

For some reason she also suggests to me that there is no

limit to energy, that there are sources of energy generated simply by spending. Of course, she may be just reflecting me back to myself. In that case, she is a vast consumer market and I can be the producer.

This is baloney. Uncle.

Mr. Pelham dropped in today. He hasn't been in for a while. In fact, the last time I saw him was the third Sunday. He asked me if I'd had any new thoughts about Ann Morr. Before I could answer, he said, "It's always seemed to me that attractive women who lived alone could be divided into two categories— those who turned into animals and those who turned into plants. Now, obviously Connie Wentz is something feline or serpentine, however clichéd that may seem. And Eleanor"— the mystery writer—"is a heron. But is it obvious that Ann is a plant? I mean, at first view one thinks of what? There is that initial post-Gibson-girl aura. When daisies replaced roses. What was that song? 'A long-stemmed American Beauty rose.' But I put it to you: Is it not possible that she is in fact not a flower but a butterfly camouflaged as one?"

I interrupted to say that this sounded like one of the Sunday-afternoon games.

He said, "Yes, it was, in fact. Ann was really quite pleased with her floral aspect. Someone said peony, someone hydrangea, and so forth. I said, 'And now to reveal the worm in the bud.' Surprisingly enough, it was Connie Wentz who rose to defend her. Connie said that *I* was the worm in the bud, if I wanted to know what I was. I imagine if you had been there you would have been the one to rise up in gallantry. I may say, one of the great pleasures of having you come round on Sundays is seeing the flowering of your gallantry toward Ann. A really unsuspected fineness—I hope you're not offended if I say that. It gives me great pleasure. Of course, it gives her great pleasure too."

It's funny they should both have said "gallant." Just because she's forty-nine doesn't mean I'm gallant. I'm not doing a favor. I'm not putting on manners. I'm not doing anything I don't want.

Four Sundays have gone by. I asked Mrs. Morr to go to the theater. I hadn't really thought what it would be like marching up to her door solo. But it didn't bother me too much. In a way, I didn't have to worry so much about guidelines for this case.

She was wearing a dress that was low cut, not all around but with a narrow V that went down to the top of her stomach. I said, "Heads will turn at that."

She said, "I should hope so." And then, "I once had a dressmaker, a very talented little man, who said to me, 'My dear, when you pass forty, you either retreat or rally.'"

I suppose I should have said she'd certainly rallied, but what was interesting was the feeling of her talking in her drawing room way and all the while it was just the two of us standing in the elevator. I was very conscious of the echo of her chatter and the fact of just the two of us standing in the elevator.

But we had a pretty good time when she ran down a little and was just asking questions. And then she has a few essays too. Even when she's not trying hard, though, she reminds me of a row of game booths at a county fair. Every place you look there's something arranged. And every time you win a game you get a souvenir trinket.

I dropped in on her and got to talk for a while. She ended up in an odd mood. She was playing music on the phonograph, and she suddenly started in talking in a different way.

"I remember when I was eighteen—I'd just got out of

boarding school and I was staying with my best friend, whose name was Sally. Sally had a sixteen-year-old brother who was terribly attractive, but of course two years at that stage was an unthinkable barrier to serious consideration, or what we took to be serious consideration. If we'd only known. But I played tennis with him and so forth until one night at supper Sally said to him, 'Go on, tell her. If you don't, I'll tell her something worse.' The poor boy was very embarrassed and wouldn't tell. I don't think I've seen that kind of paralyzing embarrassment for years now; maybe it's no longer culturally possible. In any case, it finally came out that all it was was that he'd said to Sally that he thought I looked like Ginger Rogers. I did, rather. I probably still do; I hope she's aged gracefully. But I was flattered, and I remember feeling a glow of satisfaction and, oddly enough, a sense of power. It's the feeling of power that I remember, because I think it molded me. I smiled at him—I wish I could remember his name—I smiled what I see now as an awful simper, and said, 'Do you think Ginger Rogers is pretty?' He was just too young to carry it off or slide away from it—I mean, he could have said, 'As blonds go' or 'If you like bony shoulders,' but he was pinned and could only say yes— although it took him, oh, a minute, which of course made it worse for him. I may have cooed him along by saying something like 'I'll be just *finished* if you don't think she is,' but the minute was mostly a thick silence. Until he said yes. And then somehow I was intrigued by his suffering, and also his vitality in a way—if you see what I mean—and I managed to end up on the terrace with him just before dark, just the two of us. I remember how green everything was, so it must have been still somewhat light, but it was dark enough so that I couldn't see him actually blush. He was leaving to spend the summer in Maine the next day, and I said there must be someone who was going to miss him, being gone for so long—some special friend. He said no. And I said, 'Well, I know *some*one who's going to miss you.' He said, 'Who?' I didn't say anything, and I could

feel him teetering on the brink of understanding. I knew he
wasn't slow—I knew *I* had made him a little dumb. I could feel
it. And then I felt completely what he felt when he did understand. I felt his whole terrific crush on me become concentrated
right there. In fact, it scared me a little. I knew all I had to do
was touch him, even just on the arm, and he would— Actually,
now I'm not sure what he would have done. I think at the time
I thought he would fall on his knees and worship me, saying,
'You're beautiful and perfect,' and that was more than I could
manage. I mean his *saying* it—his thinking it was perfectly all
right." Ann laughed. "What stuck with me, though, wasn't so
much the contriving aspect of it finally. It was an appreciation
of tenderness. Not sentimental tenderness. I mean tenderness in
a way I can really only describe in terms of texture. Small
white asparagus. And newness, like putting the first mark on
the first page of a book of blank pages. I think that experience
did much more to me than it did to him. I think he probably
caught a fish, or won a sailboat race, and was able to counter-
weight it, but it turned me into an appreciator, it made me
aware of how aloof you must be to really taste. Like Charles—
it makes me wonder if Charles had an experience like that. It's
odd that he and I never get as rhapsodically recollective with
each other as we do with other people. I've never told this to
anyone. I haven't thought of it while I've been with anyone is
probably why. But what is curious is that I think the really
molding experiences come much later than one is told they do.
Not at three or four or in the womb or whenever, but right on
the brink of being grown up. I'm really not that different now
than I was then. I mean, of course I am. I'm . . . older." She
laughed again. "The sadder but wiser girl. No, neither one. But
you're sweet to listen." She touched my cheek with her hand
and then got up to change the record, which hadn't shut itself
off automatically.

Her telling me that, which she hasn't told anyone else,
made a big difference to me. I also think she's right about

formative experiences. The mind has no power to direct one's life before a certain age. The really formative experiences are just as the mind begins to get that power and lurches forward.

I'm not sure that was her basic point. It's hard to sort out her basic points sometimes. They run together.

I threw Mr. Pelham for a loss today. He came in to chat and was just about to start in when I said, "I need your advice about something. I'd like to get Mrs. Morr a present and I can't think what."

He stood there awhile. He finally said, "I must say, I really can't say. And what an opportunity gone by. An occasion for a Lord Chesterfield letter to his son. 'On choosing a present for . . . an older woman.' There must be some general principles."

I said, "An example or two would do."

He said, "As Sir Philip Sidney may or may not have been the first to say, 'Let your heart be your guide.' Actually, I don't agree with that. There should be a tension between feeling and cleverness."

"What did you give her last Christmas?"

"Hmm. A book. A book about French furniture."

I said, "I don't think she needs any more books."

He said, "I'm not prepared. There is an essay here, but I'm not prepared to give it."

I said, "That's O.K. I'm not in a rush."

He said, "The moment has come and gone."

I said, "She once went on about a book of blank pages, but whether she meant a sketchbook or a diary, I don't know."

He said, "I couldn't say."

I suppose it was inevitable, or at least obviously probable, but the issue always seemed to me in doubt, or at least unforeseeable in any detail.

I suppose there was even some fear on my part that some-how, in spite of my being attracted, there would be something unattractive, some sign of age that would put me off. But when I kissed her it was exactly like kissing a girl.

I don't know why I always believed everything I heard about sex. From a very early age I took the most preposterous things on faith, in spite of the fact that I was otherwise skeptical and inquisitive. I suppose there was very little that was sensual in my life. My mental taboos just fell in with the obvious physi-cal ones—don't touch, don't think. I remember at a bus station once I watched a three-year-old boy handle his mother's breast, and I thought something had happened. I mean something up-setting for everyone there. Nothing had.

Someone told me that John Locke had said, "I owe my powers of logic to the fact that I have never loosed a drop of semen." I didn't question it, although I didn't buy half of what he said about politics or money. Everything else I'd heard and accepted re sex seemed as absurd, but true. No. Maybe just not to be considered. Not to be tied in with anything else.

I remember in college a guy down the hall slept with a professor's wife who was much older, and the whole prospect of it seemed so beyond anything thinkable that I thought at first, along with everyone else, that it wasn't true. I think there was something that shocked the guy who did it too, so that he had to minimize it by telling his dorm buddies. It took him a while to convince everyone that he really had. Then finally someone asked, "Hey, well, what was it like?" The guy said, "Applesauce!" Mainly to get back on top now that we believed him. It was about that time that I read in a history book about the Donner Pass cannibalism, and the two stories seemed equally well reported, equally verified, but equally unthinkable in terms of anyone's real flesh. In fact, the only thing I remember as creating any recognizable connection be-tween my flesh and the flesh in the Donner party was cold. For about a week whenever I went outside I'd trudge through the snow thinking of the Donner party's flesh. It didn't occur to me that they might have cooked it.

However, nothing has changed between Ann and me in terms of the proportions of my sentiments. By that I mean that what still interests me most about her is my interest. In a sense, all that has happened is that although she had my complete attention before, and still has my complete attention, it's expanded.

It's odd, but one of the responses I have to her is very much like being called on my first year in law school and not being quite prepared. After a long while of dreading this feeling, I grew to look forward to it. It struck my whole system like a shot. Sudden jolts of clarity. A struggle to hold them against the oppression of the silence that followed my name being called. A struggle to hold them against the inevitable contentiousness of all the big-mouths who happened to be primed for that class. At least there's not that aspect. But there often are the jolts of clarity out of a half fear.

And perhaps there is a fear of change. That I will change in a way that I myself will not be able to follow. That, too, was a first-year-law-school fear. An almost physical sensation that a professor would fit a wrench to a part of my mind and give it a quick half turn. And then everything would change in a way that would leave me behind. Of course, I was wrong about that; there was nothing that mysterious going on. And I got over it. But I grew to like the fear of being called on; I grew to use those jolts almost like flares to light up that part of the case that I hadn't got by myself.

But what am I lighting up when I get these jolts from Ann?

Ann changes the sheets on her bed every day. I'm sure of it not just because of how it feels but because the sheets are often different colors. Some of them are striped.

·   ·   ·

Yesterday (Sunday) Ann and I took the day off. The feeling that we should have been with the usual gang plus guests made the time seem more valuable. At least concentrated. Even though we didn't actually do anything. We got up late, ate breakfast, played music. Ann gave me dancing lessons. Different old-fashioned dances—Charleston, tango. A lot of clowning around. We sat down tired out.

Odd conversation No. 1: She said, "What is your dream career?"

"You mean like being President?"

"Oh, well, that. But I mean something more specifically dreamlike. You don't dream of being President. Do you? Something like winning the World Series."

"Yeah, I used to dream of being discovered by a Red Sox scout when I was in high school. But I couldn't have been too serious, I didn't even play freshman ball at college. What about you?"

"Oh, endless lists. Dancing with the Bolshoi. Going to the moon. Stealing the Hope diamond. Starring in a movie. Playing the organ in a cathedral."

"You could get that all into one if you tried. Star in a movie about a lady who plays the organ, steals the Hope diamond, and stashes it on the moon. On the way back you crash-land in Siberia and get discovered by the Bolshoi. I could arrive on a baseball tour, and it ends with us looking at the moon trying to figure out a way to get the diamond back."

She said, "You don't have much feel for dreams. They can't have denouements. They have to stop in the middle. At the fullest moment. There has to be a feeling of risk still clinging to the dream even when it's over. You really should think more about your dreams."

I said, "It's just another word game. This way, I mean. I don't have anything against real dreams."

She frowned and went off to change, since we'd talked about going out for lunch. When she goes to change, it can

mean anything, including taking a bath and reading the *Times*.
I turned on the Giants-Packers game. I started to turn it off
when she got back, but she wanted to watch it. At half time she
got up and did an imitation of the drum majorettes. She can be
very funny clowning around. But for some reason in the middle of it she must have thought I wasn't laughing, or was laughing too much. I don't know. She stopped and I got up and
without saying a word we were somehow squaring off over
nothing.

She finally said, "I'm sure it's ridiculous. I'm sure you think
I shouldn't make a fool of myself."

I didn't say anything, and she kept on glowering at me. I
still didn't see why I had to say anything. Then suddenly she
went into her bedroom. I went in after a bit and she told me to
get out. I went back and watched the rest of the ball game. I
felt lousy, but I couldn't apologize over nothing. When the
game was over I went in again and said, "I'm sorry."

She said, "It's terrible, but I can't do it. I hate to deprive
you of it—I mean that sweetness of a first quarrel, and the
relief that it's—but there it is. I don't feel anything but bored
with myself."

That left me to solve the problem, and I realized that she
expects a lot. More than whatever conventions she's used to—
sort of super-conventions, meta-conventions. But then maybe it
will just turn out that she wants everything left up to her.

We finally got around to lunch, which was a relief. And
then she began to giggle over how hungry I was. I am no
impediment to whatever mood she wants. There are no principles governing her change of moods. There is no control that
I feel I have, whereas she can make me feel, for example, desire
in such a concentrated form that it is almost grim, and all the
while she can keep on talking, laughing, knowing that she is
drawing me, and not the other way around.

And yet this arrangement is in no way draining or degrading. We are equals, taken over all. At least that is my impression.

Later in the day she said, "I suppose the reason I have dream careers and you don't is that I have a real regret that I haven't really done something. Something absolutely apart from myself. Something that other people use. Isn't that why you work so hard? Of course, Charles worked hard, and he still wishes he'd done something else."

I said, "Mr. Pelham's a little bit nuts."

She said, "I must say, Charlie, you're getting awfully disrespectful in your old age."

Later that evening she was smoking in bed. She smokes like a chimney. She wants me to too. She says it would make her feel very intimate to lie around and contaminate our lungs together.

She said, "What exactly is your vision of your ambition? I mean, what form does it take symbolically? Do you count the names over yours on the letterhead and imagine yours moving upward year by year?"

"I'm not on the letterhead. The youngest partner is just forty."

"Ah. But what do you think of concretely? Your name on the door of some massive office? Some particular person deferring to you?"

"No."

She waited for me to say more. She nudged me. "You're like a hostile witness. That is the phrase, isn't it? Well then, what feelings do you have about yourself ten years from now?"

"I don't know. It's not that clear. I sometimes get a feeling of weight, thinking about being the only person qualified to take on a certain kind of problem. That's not the answer, is it? You want me to have a plot of some kind to make myself number-one something or other, but that's not it. I'm not playing, I'm not making a movie of my life. I'm just working. I know you'd like to hear something more exciting."

"I stand rebuked."

"No. I don't mean it that way. But it does make me feel strange when you bring up that idea, the idea that I should have some vision, be able to hover above it all, ready to swoop down for the prize. In fact, I don't know but that all bird's-eye views aren't wrong. The world laid out to plan. It's not. Even if it were, it wouldn't be made up of stories. The only way you can be sure you're worth something is when someone thinks you're necessary, when someone needs you to make something work. Then you know."

"And all the unnecessary people are just . . . unnecessary."

"I'm talking about what I know, about what I *can* know. The rest is just emotion."

"I must say I find you very exasperating in this mood. I didn't realize you were so self-centered."

"You're missing the point. I'm just using myself as an example of the only way it makes sense to look at a career. You asked the question about me in the first place."

"It really won't do, you know," she said. "I mean, every time you find yourself . . . in any way touched, you rush back to your office and start arguing. It just won't do. You'll never grow up to be a real live boy, Pinocchio, if you act like that."

We lay awake, and much later she said she was sorry. I said I was more exhausted at the end of that day than if I'd worked all day. She said she was glad. Then she said she was so tired she couldn't sleep. She went and took a sleeping pill. Just as she was dozing off she said, "I wonder who you'll marry—what she's like." That woke me up completely, but Ann dozed off with her pill.

III

I wonder still about what sort of feelings she has for me. I'm sure it is more than just reassurance. Certainly the feelings I have for her vary, but at their most intense they are real spurts of admiration that fuse all my other feelings.

Last Sunday I went to the group meeting with her again. There was a foreigner there who had come with Professor Keller. The man was even fatter than Herr Doktor Keller (as Ann calls him) and came from Central Europe someplace. Not Hungary, but somewhere near it. Now an American citizen. He was being treated very respectfully by everyone. Alleged brains? Influence? Still don't know. He told the following story:

"In 1937 I visited—in my capacity as private economist— the head of one of the oldest families in Hungary. I do not mention the name, but you may imagine. I went to one of his several country estates. As we traveled over roads which you in this country cannot imagine—almost impassable—I said, 'Excellency, how far to your estate?' 'My friend,' he said, 'we have been on my estate for an hour now.' We traveled for another hour, passing several villages which were more squalid than anything you have in this country. Squalor and penury beyond anything you can conceive, I assure you. We arrived at the hunting lodge, which was palatial. There was a vast courtyard, however, which was a bog, solid mud up to the thighs. I started to descend from the car, but my host stopped me. Two servants rushed from the nearest door and floundered toward us. They carried us on their backs to the steps of the lodge. They struggled through the mud like beasts of burden. It's not something that you in this country can easily imagine. That evening I took my host aside to speak with him. I said, 'Excellency, you have asked me to advise you. I may, however, be overstepping the bounds of my service when I say to you something from my deepest convictions. The conditions of life in this country are by modern standards unbearably harsh. It is no longer the nineteenth century. You have already experienced a first upheaval, which I assure you was more than the effect of losing a war. There must be either reform or upheaval. You are in an exceptional position. I beg you with great earnestness—I implore you, before it is too late—invest what you can of your fortune in the American market.' "

Ann began to giggle. No one else batted an eye. The man went on, "But he failed to listen to me. He did nothing to avert the financial disaster that overtook his entire family. It was a blindness that you cannot imagine in this country."

Ann burst out laughing.

Professor Keller said quickly, "But his holdings in this country would have been sequestered during the war in any case."

The man said, "I had in mind a holding company based in a neutral country."

Ann kept on laughing. Even Mr. Pelham gave her a look. She was laughing very loudly by this time. Mr. Pelham was always alarmed by loudness. But it was her being loud and rude that I really loved. I'd been trying to think of something to say, but she was much better. And what was good was that she was out of control. She wasn't picking away at this guy; she couldn't help it. Her eyes squinted up and her mouth was open so wide I could see her gold fillings in the back. I wanted to get her away and just listen to her laugh.

I missed the turn the conversation took, but things broke up fairly soon after. We went back to her place, but the mood had passed, and she in fact seemed somber, so I wasn't able to tell her she'd been terrific. It doesn't matter; she was.

Answer [Mr. Pelham]: "Certainly. What it is that I find in my social life is this: That the threads of my life (ideas, friends, et al.) are woven into designs around me of course interests me, but what interests me more is when I can feel the threads being pulled out by a neighbor's design in the making—being stolen inch by inch, sliding out of their backing, over and under and over and under and finally out. Well, that is a sensation that is certainly worth more to me than the jealous retention of the designs in my own life. What is best of all, by the way, is to feel several designs being raveled away multifariously. I feel very much in touch then, as they ravel out of my life and are knitted up into several others. It is, if you will allow a certain dryness [*laughter*] or aridity of phrase, a sociospiritual sensation. Which gives me great pleasure."

Q: "Pleasure?"

A: "Satisfaction. Fulfillment. It is, you know. I should add that people always talk of sacrifice wrongly. The word once meant a pleasurable giving. Now it means, oh, rationing, privation, imposition. People then turn around and say, e.g., Proust sacrificed his life for his work. I would assert that on the contrary, Proust was not in the least deprived but very cleverly bargained away a life that he could never have really led for one that gave him the highest pleasure. I would be happy to make—in a very minor way, you understand—the same sort of bargain."

Q: "What in exchange for what?"

A: "What I can't have for what I've decided I really want."

Q: "Who are you dealing with?"

A: "Well, let's call it a broadside offer."

Q: "Well, what can't you have?"

A: "Earlier expectations."

Q: "Like what?"

A: "Well, to lead you somewhat astray, to be a national figure."

Q: "Seriously?"

A: "Yes. There was a moment."

Q: "But your earlier expectations—i.e., what you can't have—are they yours to bargain with?"

A: "I can't think who else can claim them."

Q: "Of course, if they're what you can't have, they're

without value and your bargain is *nudum pactum,* without consideration."

A: "I tell you they're extremely valuable. All that I once cared for."

Q: "But if you're going to give up what you can't have, you're bargaining to do something you're bound to in the first place—"

A: "Put that way, of course, there is some merit to your objection. But not in my life. The logic in my life has not been law. [*Laughter*] In fact, in this realm everyone is always making bargains to do what he's already bound to do. Those are the only ones anyone sticks to."

Q: " 'In this realm.' Everything just slips away."

A: "Oh, no. . . . You know, it's a shame we're the only two lawyers or we could do this some Sunday."

Ann: "You know, I was struck today by the helplessness one feels in front of what is most touching. Last summer I was at a family picnic, of all things. I have a nephew named Bill who is a great ox of a schoolboy who spends all his time exercising, as far as I can see, and I have a cousin once removed who is sixteen and quite attractive. She has a little brother of an indeterminate age named Josh. Perhaps he's eight, or six. All three happened to be standing by the swimming pool. My cousin had a great crush on this lifeguard of a nephew—why, I can't imagine—and she was trying to attract his attention. So she started talking to her little brother. 'If you'll go swimming with me, Josh, I'll give you a surprise.' Josh said, 'What?' He was—quite rightly—suspicious of this sudden bright-eyed attention. My cousin said, 'Oooh, I can't tell you, but it'll be something you really, really like.'

"Josh still said 'What?' but what intrigued me was that he was beginning to squirm under the intensity of her really remarkable physical charm. She was hovering over him, and although she wasn't touching him, the air was positively electric, and of course he couldn't know it wasn't for him. All the while Bill was doing deep-breathing exercises of some laborious sort. Finally my cousin turned to Bill and said, 'Oh, Bill. You make him come swimming with me. He's just being awful.' Josh looked very hurt that he was being awful, but Bill said, 'Can't talk. Hyperventilating,' and then dove into the pool and swam underwater down and back. It's quite a long pool, and he pulled himself out like a wounded crocodile and just lay in the sun, occasionally rearing his head to knock the water out of his ear. My cousin looked down at him for a while with that brutal sour look that teen-agers have, which I hope is not as seriously evil as it looks. Then she walked off. Bill just lay there oblivious. Josh wandered around the pool looking very thin and sorry for himself, but when I talked to him he was completely bored and couldn't wait for me to stop."

An odd thing. Mr. Pelham and Ann both happened to ask me the same question.

Mr. Pelham: "I imagine there is such a thing as rustic virtue. Disabuse me."

Ann: "You must have had a marvelous childhood—I mean, growing up away from all the usual vices. Catching trout while boys in New York were shoplifting. Everything must have been so natural."

I said to Ann, "There's nothing more natural about New Hampshire than New York anymore. Most of those trout are stocked. My brother worked as a guard at a state trout hatchery. Herons would come in droves to eat the hatch and he'd shoot the herons by the dozens. *They* were what was *natural*. But it's an economic election. Herons or trout. Tourists come for trout. Q.E.D." Ann was appalled.

I said to Mr. Pelham that if rusticity itself is the virtue he's talking about, and if virtue is desirable, which we assert by definition, then why did I, and my fellows, come to New York, and why does the rest of the state want, more than rusticity, electric power, highways, industry? And so forth.

Story for story, essay for essay. But I begin to think that their idea of the purpose of their relations with other people is primarily informational. And that eventually the information, the more interested they become, will be an essence of me that they'll have to dismantle me to get. Nothing necessarily destructive. Just to see. I suppose that's O.K.

I asked Mr. Pelham how he'd ever come to drop in, what first interested him. He wasn't surprised. He had his essay.

"I thought at first you were—from what people said—what every rigorous headmaster of every rigorous prep school claimed he wanted his boys to be. In practice, headmasters were often thrown into violent reactions by factors they professed to ignore. E.g., charm. They were both infatuated and irritated by it. But the theory of their preaching was that 'a strong character' was to be praised over intelligence, charm, talent, and even accomplishment. It was a curious thing to preach, because it was a sermon without end that crushed everyone. It praised, for example, those who gave their lives for their country in a way which made the living feel guilty. It praised the grit of the loser who battled on and on. Hopelessly. Which made the winner feel guilty and was no balm to the loser, because even when one is told he has a strong character, one cannot really acknowledge it inwardly. In any event, praise of one's grit should be no substitute for winning.

"A curious side effect of this preaching, by the way, was that certain extremely gifted prep school boys competing some years later for, let us say, Rhodes Scholarships would falter almost on purpose before the interviewing committee. They were under a posthypnotic suggestion, you see, to lose with grit and prove their character.

"But to return to you. You seemed to be slogging it out on your own in both theory and practice, and because no one had imposed the theory on you, you were uninhibited toward bald success. I can't tell you how deep a chord this struck in me. I have often had a dream career of being a headmaster. To be quasi-Olympian above the fray. To be on the riverbank as a racing eight swept by, knowing the life story of each man in the boat. What each stroke cost." He paused. "To bestow the trophy, saying, 'Well rowed, Prancer and Dancer and Donder and Blitzen . . .' "

Later I asked Ann what had first got her interested in me. She started to back away, but I finally got the bit in her mouth. And then, of course, she took it between her teeth and ran off.

"Well, I can say one thing, which is that you're unlike any previous entanglement. Except perhaps Charles. Charles was like you—many years ago, of course. Not in manner. But he was isolated in the same way. Nothing, I can tell you, is less appealing than a lonely man who is feeling sorry for himself, but on the other hand, a lonely man who seems to be bearing up and who acts with a certain rudeness is infinitely attractive. The only thing more momentarily alluring—and it can be only momentary—is a man who is obviously in love with another woman, who is paying absolutely no attention to anything else, and who then, out of a clear blue sky, suddenly notices you and is visibly shaken. It's quite moving. But then, of course, he must either turn away sheepishly or advance raffishly, and that is that. I'm afraid I may be sounding like a terrible old whore, but if you insist on questions, I'm afraid you'll get answers that go on like this. I mean, I'm not going to pretend that I returned to my maidenly role as frail flower after Alfred departed the scene. Indeed, I don't even think that I find it a convincing role—frail flower, I mean. It is aesthetically repugnant, and I may say I'm glad to see that it is really not even a fashion anymore. Which is not to say that I admire myself unreservedly. In fact, I was somewhat unreflective with Charles in that it should have been apparent to me that since he was someone whom Alfred admired a great deal, I very likely had ulterior motives. I have noticed that divorced women tend either toward someone whom their husbands admire or toward someone whom their husbands rather despise. A visible step up or down. From the husband's point of view, of course. The reality is always more baffling. But the original motive is to break away from the husband's taste in people, which is the most lingering shared taste, because, of course, the people around you can't be sent into storage along with certain chairs and rugs and paintings. But the people can be perceived differently. And one changes oneself, and so forth, until there is a whole new arrangement. But the period of changing one's perceptions is, oddly, a very impersonal one—although not necessarily rational—and the person closest to one at the time gets treated rather badly, I'm afraid. That is to say, impersonally. I mean, one can behave quite theoretically. Women can. Men on the whole behave better, more naturally, at least more wholeheartedly. Alfred behaved extremely wholeheartedly and remarried very happily, if a little bit absurdly.

"Fortunately Charles and I became lasting friends, largely through his withdrawal in a very independent and orderly fashion. There was scarcely a bad moment. We were both very busy, and we soon found that we weren't relying on each other at all, even though we kept on seeing each other. This was years ago. And then, of course, he became more the way he is now. His whole world in his head. Not in any selfish or even embittered way. Perhaps a little melancholy, but very literary, very picturesque. What I find attractive now is that he is analytic in a generous way, but not a and b, x and y—like a juggler, really, so that you just catch a glimpse. It really is the way I prefer to hear about things."

I said, "I guess you find me too much the other way. Too *x* and *y*."

She said, "Now, that is the intriguing thing; I really don't know. Actually I do—at least one thing, which is this: that you're changing visibly, and I find it amazing to be a cause— not so much a cause as a catalyst. Do you know what happens to catalysts, by the way? People are always using catalyst as a metaphor, and I know what it means metaphorically, but actu- ally, chemically, I have no idea what happens to them.

"Do you remember saying that your sleek, demure young associates seemed to know you down to the ground and that you didn't know the first thing about them? I can assure you that that is most unlikely. There is, to flatter you some, some- thing awesome about you. I'm quite serious. You really are as independent as Charles was, but with a more massive core of energy. Of course, that may be youth. I'll tell you what I do like, though, is that from time to time you seem to focus it all on me. I can't tell you how I've come to appreciate that feeling. Wasn't that what you wanted to know?"

I said yes.

She said, "You know, for someone who never mentions it, you're actually quite sensual."

She smiled, having deliberately turned the conversation that way. I noticed her mouth particularly. Her front teeth are large and regular. There is something attractive about the idea of her gold fillings in back, on the way to her red gullet. I find myself sometimes thinking about her insides, almost in a way to put me off. Not on account of her but on account of my own state of mind. The other day it made me think of shooting a deer—the whole process—seeing it flash, shooting, hauling it out, gutting it. Other times, fortunately, I think of her bones. They're very light, and that is altogether pleasant, associated mainly with her control of her body.

I have mentioned the deer to her, making it clear that that

edge of thought exists only involuntarily. She said it probably had to do with my resenting the fact that she could not have a baby. I said no, that her steering clear of babies made her seem more like a young girl.

She said, "A quick-frozen young girl, thawed out in perfect condition years later."

I didn't say anything, but the fact is I'm not sure I would have liked her as a young girl. What I like is that she seems like a young girl. She, on the other hand, is in love with her memories of being a girl. I doubt if I'll ever spend that much time dredging up stories. My story, the one that interests me, is from now on.

It is interesting how Ann can tell stories publicly (the way she did today, Sunday) with real polish. And then she can tell me a story in private as though her recollections were a form of caress, as though she were nestling against me. If she were a patient and I were a psychiatrist, I would fall in love with her as she just lay there talking. She sometimes demands stories from me, but that is often like a caress that she asks for. Too requested. She once took my hand and very slowly pulled it against her face; now, if she could get stories from me like that . . .

But when I hear her tell a story in public, it is hard to imagine how we ever get along in private. I can imagine what it would be like to be married to an actress.

Today Professor Keller got after her about laughing at his Central European "private economist." She said, "Let me explain. Marie-Claire was being driven back to her villa in Neuilly by her chauffeur when she happened to see a tramp eating grass by the roadside. She rapped on the glass partition and told the chauffeur to stop. She addressed the tramp. 'My good man,' she said. 'Are you actually eating grass by the roadside?' The tramp said, 'Yes, madame.' 'Well then, you must come with me,' said Marie-Claire. They drove off and at length reached Marie-Claire's house. She told the tramp to follow her. They proceeded through the front hall, and out the back door onto the terrace. Marie-Claire gestured with her slim white hand across the well-tended grounds. 'My poor fellow,' she said. 'I was touched when I saw you eating grass by the roadside. *Here* is an English lawn!' "

Professor Keller said, "Oh, come on. That's not an analogy." But Ann won the point by acclamation.

I enjoy her triumphs, but not as much as she does. She lights up, revs up, and doesn't slow down for hours. But when she does finally, she is especially low-keyed and balmy. When we got back to her place I was going to leave, but she said no—she wanted me to sit and talk for a while. She floated around the living room, turning on lights in corners and bringing me a drink. She settled down on the sofa and said, "I've been thinking about that friend of yours you told me about."

I said I didn't remember any more than the first time I told her. She said, "That's all right. Tell me again. I love it. It's like a painting."

I told her again. "I had a friend in New Hampshire who lived outside Nashua when he was a kid, and he started going to a whore in town when he was just fourteen. He would save up his chore money, and when he had ten bucks, which was maybe every other month, he'd go down to see this whore, who mostly just did the old geezers around town—the retired mill hands and so forth. She was always very glad to see him, and she would give him a bath and ask him how he was doing in school and on the baseball team and so forth—the same things each time—and then she'd dry him off, take off her bathrobe, get up on the bed, and say, 'Climb aboard, sunshine boy.' "

"Tell me when he told you," Ann said. "How did it come up? How old was he?"

"When he told me? We were both eighteen, and he hadn't told anyone before me. After we got out of high school we got a couple of IDs and went to the dog races down in Taunton. In the last race there was a dog named Sunshine Boy, and my friend started laughing and told me about it. We went out to a bar and had some drinks, and he couldn't get off it. It was the first time I'd seen anybody drunk that way, although he was probably copying someone he'd seen. At the time I couldn't tell if it was real. He said something like 'She's probably dead and gone.' He fell asleep in the car and I drove back to New Hampshire. I went off the next day to a summer job in Keene and then to college. He joined the Army, I think. I used to think about that in college—his story, I mean. It seemed mysterious. Not so much the sex part—that seemed more natural than anything else I heard—but the fact that he'd kept it secret for such a long time and finally only told me by accident."

Ann said, "It is like a Hopper. A cliché imbued with realism. A realized cliché. An intensified cliché. No. You aren't making anything up?"

I said no.

She said, "What I like about Hopper is this—the other dimension, the suggested dimension, is absolutely, precisely in focus. There is nothing to play with, to jiggle into focus. It all comes at once. In fact, it all comes at once even though I don't know of another painter who can suggest that a scene—the one of the inside of the movie theater, for instance—has such a stretch of long, boring time locked into it. Just on and on and on. Even his houses with the yards grown over. And yet every one of his paintings has such a clear point. I mean, all the time is brought to a head, as though his picture is a dam waiting for you to look at it for all the time to be released."

I thought: This is the way she is most coherent—fitting her mood to a subject and controlling both at once by talking. I thought: I have never known anyone this well and this abstractly at the same time. Somehow she has made sure I know the mechanics of her, but for no mechanical reason.

At the same time, I thought that we were caught up then

too, sitting there and drifting in her mood. I thought it would not be possible for us to feel this way if she were not completely *for* me.

I V

Mr. Pelham got back today. He's been away for two weeks or so, so I haven't seen him since Ann told me their ancient history. At first it bothered me a little, but then I thought that, after all, he's over sixty now, and there might as well be a statute of limitations on that sort of thing.

In any case he was very subdued. No essay on France, where he'd been. He asked me if I knew that Ann was taking a trip to France and I said no, but that it didn't surprise me, since she went every spring. Then he asked me how I was doing on the job, and I said O.K., although that is something he could certainly find out better from one of the other partners. Then he just mumbled around for a while. Not one of his brighter days. But I have to ask myself, Am I faster now to pick him up on signs of bleariness? Do I *try* to see him as gone by?

I have changed some, at least in one respect. My "ear," as Ann—or Mr. Pelham—would say, is attuned.

Ann told me this: "If you are ever miserable, Charlie, I can tell you that you shouldn't despise Job's comforters. I remember when Alfred and I were divorced, which was a perfectly good idea, but nevertheless a painful experience—like a physical illness—an aunt of mine, who was an extremely kind and silly woman, took me to lunch and comforted me. She said, 'Ann, my dear, it was really too perfect. Too good to be true. You were both too glamorous, you know. I mean, it was just too perfect and unreal for you to keep your minds on each other. What you really needed was someone less high-powered. He was too ambitious to give you the kind of attention that would nurture you. You simply weren't nurtured, because he never gave a thought to it. I remember saying something like this to you some time ago. I'm sure you don't remember, because there was no way you could have understood at the time. I'm not saying I could have saved you any unhappiness, but it was just so clear to someone outside, to someone who really wanted you to be happy. And I hope you will be, dear.' Of course, she was nowhere near right. If anyone ever insisted on nurturing, on the hothouse, green-thumb approach to wives, it was Alfred. I assure you, his current wife would win a tulip contest in Holland. But everything my aunt said was strangely comforting. It made the whole subject seem remote. Something that I knew more about than anyone in the world but that was essentially a very obscure, useless subject. Something it would do me no good to think about anymore but that I was satisfied to have figured out.

"And my aunt took me to have my hair done and bought me some new clothes, all of which was so beside the point, but helpful. In fact, I think I cut my hair short the next week. But my aunt's carrying on reminded me that there was a ritual, and that where there is a ritual there must be a midden of old experience nearby, and that I could just go on for a while impersonally until I felt like taking over myself again."

Some time after Ann told me this, I realized that it could be construed as advice, and even as fair warning.

I'd never seen a steel mill. It's a good thing I went through after the conference. I couldn't have got it out of my mind when I laid out the memos for the various company officers. It would have made me think there must be more to them than there really is.

Mr. Leland got sick. I went to Pittsburgh by myself. Scared the hell out of me. Even though I knew that I knew what they wanted to know.

The client's v.p. who was in charge of setting up the conference had written to Mr. Leland that it would be O.K. for Mr. Leland to send his second-in-command. I guess the v.p. figured that with the money they pay us, there must be at least a half dozen old gray lawyers working full time. So when I walked into his office the v.p. assumed I was the second-in-command's clerk. His mistake aggravated me some, since I was nervous. However, I soon realized he was a jerk. While he was still a little embarrassed and thought maybe I just looked young, he actually asked my age. I said, "Twenty-seven going on twenty-eight." He didn't even smile. His secretary laughed and then he managed to get it.

I laid out the issues for them without much trouble. At first I thought one of them was laying some elaborate groundwork with his questions, but it turned out he was just a little slow. After that the only thing that surprised me was how much dead wood they carry in their executives. They could get along just as well with a couple of the bright ones. And then I guess I was surprised at how conservative they were even just discussing, or rather not discussing, litigation. They moaned once or twice about the cost of litigation, even though that should be peanuts to them.

But the tour of the steel mill impressed me. Oddly enough, I thought of Ann talking about what art should be concerned with—i.e., the changes that are ordinarily hidden from us. But I suppose you don't really see the transformation here, although the impression is that you do. The coal and ore coming in one side and steel being rolled out the other, and the cooling sheets visible from a catwalk. It was the colors that amazed me most. They looked like red clouds being blown across a bright moon. They seemed to have a shape and another side down in the cooling steel.

I was impressed with my response too. To the color and to the brute force of the process. It amazed me that a process so violent and precise should have a by-product as momentary and delicate as those shades of red. I admired both. And then I finally thought: Here is an analogy for Mr. Pelham: I was raw material before I went to law school. Practically useless. I was fed into the mill, and by a violent but precise process I became useful. But not until Ann and Mr. Pelham came along did I realize there were appreciable by-products, that I was not so colorless—and did not have to be so grimly thrifty with myself —as I had grown used to thinking.

But without the original crude effort there would have been much less now. Both the violent energy and its precise control served me, and they would not have worked on me so well had I been able to imagine there was any other way.

I must admit that this line of thought would not have occurred to me without the influence of Ann and Mr. Pelham, and I am going back to New York gladly. With relief to leave here. I don't have the simple single-minded drive I once had. There were dark hints here from the company—room for another house counsel, not a surprising thing for house counsel to find himself in key positions on a number of matters, and so forth and so on. That would have knocked me over not so long ago. I still don't take it lightly, but it doesn't hit all of me. I suppose the hints of the company are useful testimony of my value, but I'm not so interested anymore in my brute usefulness.

I suppose the extreme of that last position would be Mr. Pelham.

I called up Ann when I got back, but she'd already left for Europe. I was surprised, and a little worried, but then traveling, especially flying, makes her so nervous that, I suppose, she suddenly found the nerve to get on and so she just got on.

I told Mr. Pelham about the company's feeling me out. He was amused, but he took it seriously too. He asked me if I'd told Mr. Leland. I said no. I wasn't even considering the offer, so I didn't want him to think I was. Mr. Pelham told me to go ahead and tell him. He said there was always a chance that someone from the company would tell him—"Ho, ho, your boy sticks pretty close to the apron strings. No, seriously, I admire loyalty"—and so I'd better tell him first. Mr. Pelham also pointed out that even if I wasn't considering it at all, it would do Mr. Leland good to hear it.

He said, "But I'm glad you like being in a firm better. I can't imagine being house counsel. That's not really law. I must say I have come to appreciate law in my nonage. I appreciate it now even in its capacity as men's club, monastery, temple of high Protestant rite. There is a reassurance in its formality, which is, after all, not a superficial aspect of it. I'm in favor of communal formality, and mental formality. Look at the mess in which people suddenly find themselves—people who have lived solely by their own personal achievements. Those can collapse in a minute. Money, personality, taste, social life. I mean a modern social life; I suppose there was a time when family tradition provided a framework for life. The proud Don Pedro in his Spanish ruff seeking death before dishonor. Now all there is of anything approaching like magnitude is professional tradition. The rest of life is merely existential. What a wonderful word, 'merely.'

"Lately I've been considering law as magic. It's not so far off—it's all done with words, the proper spells. Think of an argument on appeal: two wizards hurling incantations at each other, until finally one of them finds the properly binding words, and—*e presto!*—the material world is rearranged in accordance with them. And lawyers are possessed by their clients' problems even more thoroughly than shamans were by their patients' evil spirits. Until the case is decided, at least.

"Perhaps we're not sorcerers so much as earthworms. The compost of the nation passes through our digestive tubes and emerges rich with nitrates. Our briefs and counselings are almost pure nitrogen. Very little is created anymore, and nothing is destroyed. Isn't that basic physics? But disposition is still a possibility, and enrichment. Of course, this is the most optimistic view."

I wonder if she planned it that way—that I would be so confused by her letter that I would have to go to Mr. Pelham to find out what was really going on. And there I'd be with Mr. Pelham, who would fill me in gradually, making sure I wouldn't choke on it. Save herself a lot of worry.

Q: "Did she know all along that this guy in France wanted to marry her?"

A: "Yes, for some time, in fact. But that is not to say she knew she wanted to marry him. Even after she'd left."

Q: "But he's old."

A: "He is one year younger than I am."

Q: "Rich and all that."

A: "Rich? Oh, surely not rich. No more than Ann—"

Q: "I don't know about Ann; I never asked."

A: "She had a settlement in lieu of alimony that was well invested over the years, and she lived a comparatively simple life, which is to say—"

Q: "That they won't be in the old folks' home."

A: "No. They'll live half the year in Paris and half the year in the country. I'm sorry I can't indulge you in the momentary satisfaction of discovering flawed motives—some venality, some despicable calculation. But I'm sure that in the long run you would prefer—"

Q: "In the long run she would have been way too old."

A: "I'm equally sure that you never held your feelings to that calculation."

That was a week ago. I've begun to care some that I made a fool of myself. Not so much that I care what Mr. Pelham thinks or even what he knows. I shouldn't have tried to find out anything. Bits of information stick in my mind, no matter what. I'll never know enough, so I'd just as soon know nothing at all.

I don't know how to take it; I can't satisfy myself by reducing it to any formal proposition. The only hypothesis that I came up with that showed me anything worthwhile was this: If I had left her, I would have felt worse.

I also suppose that she would have left out of pride within five years, in any case—even though she must have had ample grounds for believing I was fairly attracted to her beyond the original impulse, for reasons that were not only self-renewing but increasingly forceful.

I think that although she felt the imbalance between my future (far off and largely deferrable; I could stay with her for five years and still marry a girl in college) and her future (imminent and brief; if she stayed with me for five years we would have gone to more funerals than weddings)—although she felt that imbalance more keenly than I did at the time, nevertheless I think that she also sensed that the longer we went on, the more I would be the one to suffer, having no accumulation of any comparable experience to offset it with. It would have been more and more all there was to my life.

Still, all these arguments are not enough to move me very far one way or another. There really isn't anything to decide. I just run arguments through to cool off. There is some calm in just going if click then clack, click clack, click clack.

No better. I have been noting a number of unfamiliar gestures —e.g., I hold my head in my hands as though it were a separable globe, I stare at my open palm. I do find myself resisting, however. I'm perfectly capable of functioning. But it takes a certain determination to function exactly as I did before.

I have noted a good point of resistance, which is Mr. Pelham. Taking his disappointments gently and reflectively must have done a lot to make him the way he is. Of course, he was more disposed to it in the first place. Not just by education. And he's good at it. I myself would make a lousy Mr. Pelham. I will not let myself be like Mr. Pelham.

When I use the term "Mr. Pelham," I'm not sure I really know the definition. Has he made sure that nothing has its hooks in him? Or do a lot of things have their hooks in him? So that he's strung up in involuntary equilibrium?

Either way, functionally speaking, it works out that he has given up whatever drive and traction he once may have had. I haven't, even if I may be temporarily without traction.

Today Mr. Pelham offered to borrow me from Mr. Leland and to take me to Japan on one of his trips. I said no, since I'm getting back to work with some solidity, but I was grateful.

I've got back into a routine of work and exercise. It is a great help just to do everything by numbers—swim fifty laps, brush my hair a hundred strokes—and work regularly but never beyond the set time. No hanging around, no getting run down. Mere routine is very helpful. Just to keep in motion, to give some structure to what I think during the slack in my schedule.

I thought: I am like an astronaut. They might as well have shot me to the moon. I handled it, I came back the same.

Q: What was it like?

A: It was nice.

Q: Nice?

A: If you wanted to hear more details you should have sent someone like Mr. Pelham. I didn't hire out for that part of the job.

Q: We had to send someone like you. We hoped the rest would just come.

Maybe it did. Maybe it just came for the astronauts too, and we've never heard about it. I imagine they are something like me—small-town boys with B minds, who learned how.

And owe it all to learning how. Are they any different now? Are their thoughts any different? Maybe we should send someone to ask them if their thoughts are any different. Maybe we should send Mr. Pelham to ask them.

Maybe the change comes later. Maybe the time to ask them is not when they've just got back but much, much later. When they're old and making it up.

Mr. Pelham got up his nerve the other day. He said, "Have you heard anything more from Ann?"

I could have turned him down with a hard no, but something stopped me. I said, "No, have you?" and he looked a lot easier about the whole thing.

He said, "No. I wonder how she is."

I said, "I'm sure she's doing fine."

He said, "Well, I assume the best."

It came to me very strongly that I was more or less myself again but that he misses her terribly.

And so he wants to pore over everything. O.K. I don't mind. More than that—there is something about the way he looks, the way the loose skin of his throat is tucked inside his collar, the way he's slowed up.

It's not pity on my part. He is the first old man I've known who is interested in what I feel. I suppose in a way I produce for him just the same way I produce for Mr. Leland. But if there's a mutual benefit in his questions and my answers, that's only a small part of it. If it's a bargain, it's certainly not one necessary to any enterprise of mine. When he comes I feel I should take care of him, although he may not need any concern of mine—he could easily find solace in the bosom of the senior part of the firm. No, I suppose it is the closest thing I have to a moral concern. In the sense of unfounded belief. I *should* deal with this man, help keep him from something— growing coldness, slowing down. He needs to be in use, to talk

about something more than old coarse light on empty buildings, than his trips to Japan, and it seems right in some over-
reaching scheme of things that he should. But he is a com-
mentator, and appreciator, not an initiator, and so for the
moment he will use me to tell him things.

I told him about the first time Ann's maid brought her
breakfast on a tray into the bedroom and I pulled the bed
covers over my head. He thought that was funny, and he
wanted to know if Ann laughed and when she laughed—while
the maid was still there? He was interested. He said, "Another
Lord Chesterfield letter—'What to do in my lady's chamber
when the maid comes in.' Once one didn't have to notice, I
suppose. But now no one can avoid being somewhat democrat-
ically aware. It would be inhuman. I think I recommend a
pleasant smile. Not that I fault you. I mean, I understand your
solid urge for privacy, even if it's carried out with ostrich-like
futility. But the completely admirable solution is a smile. And
as for the maid—also a delicate part. What did she do?"

"She brought another tray."

He said, "Exactly. And people say there's a servant problem. Of course, she wouldn't ever work on Sunday."

I could do without his finicky lines on servants and eti-
quette, and some of his other old-nob talk, but I suppose that's
the least of the things it's too late for him to change at this
stage. What I do get along with in him is this: I think he has
always tried just as hard as I do.

In fact, I think he probably even submitted himself to the
process of being a lawyer the same way I did. For all his talk
about dream careers, he chose the one he's had. And it's held
him together pretty well, even though I suspect his life has been
lonelier than mine will be. All that's wrong now is that there
are a few loose ends. I'm sure he'll work out a few essays on the
subject. Not directly on the subject, but close enough so that
I'll be able to listen for the flaw in his well-being. Like a doctor

listening to a patient's breathing while the patient talks on about his other symptoms.

I remembered today the first time I talked back to my father. I was thirteen; he was still farming then—in his fifties. We were clearing rocks out of a field so he could mow it without losing half the teeth out of the sickle bar. My mother came down with lunch just as he picked up a big rock and swung it into the back of the truck.

She said, "You'll throw your back out worse than last year."

He was in a good mood. He said, "No; I always get some strong spells in the summer. Comes right out of here." He toed the ground.

I said, "I don't see how. It's only dirt."

My mother laughed. My father said, "Maybe so." He kept me working past sunset—himself too—and the next day his back was out.

I once regarded that kind of memory as an encumbrance, or a luxury. But my most recent process isn't as simple as the one that got me to New York in the first place; it has more to do with luxuries and encumbrances. What amazes me is that there seems to be some system in all this accumulation: a year ago I couldn't have been bothered, I couldn't have refined anything out of the uneasiness, and I probably wouldn't have understood any of what has come or gone or stayed.

A NOTE ABOUT THE AUTHOR

John Casey was born in Worcester, Massachusetts, in 1939
and educated at Harvard College, Harvard Law School, and
the University of Iowa. He is the author of a novel,
An American Romance, and of many stories that have
appeared in *The New Yorker, Harper's, Redbook, Sports
Illustrated,* and other magazines. He is the recipient of a
Guggenheim Fellowship. John Casey lives with his wife and
two children in Charlottesville, Virginia, where he teaches
English literature at the University of Virginia.

A NOTE ON THE TYPE

The text of this book was set in Intertype Garamond No. 3,
a modern rendering of the type first cut by Claude Garamond (1510–1561). Garamond was a pupil of Geoffroy
Troy and is believed to have based his letters on the Vene-
tian models, although he introduced a number of important
differences, and it is to him we owe the letter which we
know as old-style. He gave to his letters a certain elegance
and a feeling of movement that won for their creator an
immediate reputation and the patronage
of Francis I of France.

*Composed by Maryland Linotype Composition Company,
Baltimore, Maryland.
Printed and bound by
The Haddon Craftsmen, Inc., Scranton, Pa.
Typography and binding design by
Virginia Tan.*